W9-ANE-007

Tell It Like It Is

Tough Choices for Today's Teens

Tell It Like It Is

Tough Choices for Today's Teens

by

Ellen Frankel and Sarah Levine

KTAV Publishing House, Inc.
Hoboken, New Jersey

Library of Congress Cataloging-in-Publication Data

Frankel, Ellen
    Tell it like it is : tough choices for today's teens / Ellen Frankel and
Sarah Levine
        p.   cm.
    Summary: Drawing upon lessons learned from her family, Jewish
tradition, and her own sense of justice, Sarah deals with a number of social
and ethical issues during her freshman year at a private school.
    ISBN 0–88125–522–X
    [1. Conduct of life—Fiction. 2. High Schools—Fiction. 3.
Schools—Fiction. 4. Jews—United States—Fiction.] I. Levine, Sarah,
1980–   . II. Title.
PZ7.F8535Te   1995
[Fic]—dc20   95–17294
                                                                     CIP
                                                                     AC

            Manufactured in the United States of America
    KTAV Publishing House, 900 Jefferson Street, Hoboken, NJ 07030

To Les

who loves stories

Contents

I

Exposed!

I knew I shouldn't have eaten breakfast, Sarah Eisenberg told herself as she stood in front of her locker, struggling with the combination lock. In her stomach blueberries, Rice Krispies, and milk were churning wildly like seashells in an undertow.

"On your first day of school," her mother had declared as she set down a bowl and spoon on the kitchen table, "you need to eat a good breakfast. I will not have any of this anorexia non-sense now that you're starting high school!"

What a curse to be the daughter of a therapist, thought Sarah. Here I am, ready to shake off the past and begin life all over again at a new school in a new city—and Mom has to dust off her psychology degree and start practicing again, specializing in adolescents no less! If anyone from Springfield School comes to see her, I'll be ruined!

"Hey, watch where you're going!"

Sarah was abruptly shaken from her daydreaming when she collided with a huge monster of a guy with fire-engine red hair and blotchy red skin covered with craters like the surface of the moon. Coffee, doughnuts, books, and loose change flew in all directions, then clattered to the tiled floor of the wide hallway. The busy traffic of students froze in suspended animation.

Grunting, the redheaded giant looked down at the mess, then spun around to face Sarah. "What's the idea? You think you own the halls or somethin'?"

"I . . . I . . ."

"Why don't you pick on someone your own size and IQ, Wayne!"

Sarah whipped around and saw three girls about her own age standing together by a row of brown lockers. Although they were wearing pretty ordinary clothes—short black boots, jeans shorts, and tank tops—they had that special air about them that said, "We own the world." They were definitely cool. They held their well-groomed heads high, noses in the air, perfect teeth flashing self-confidence and charm. At that moment, Sarah knew that she would give anything to become their friend.

"Stay out of this, Crystal! It's none a' your business," Wayne snarled at the girl who had just spoken. "This new girl needs to learn some manners. I gotta protect Springfield's reputation."

The three girls threw back their heads and roared with laughter. Wayne glared at them, and then focused his narrowed eyes on Sarah, whose smile evaporated under his fierce gaze.

"Tell you what, Wayne," said Crystal, still snorting with laughter. "How about if Julia, Christine, and I take it upon ourselves to teach our new recruit here the laws of Springfield School? We promise to devote ourselves to the task."

Wayne eyed the three girls suspiciously, then shrugged. He bent down, scooped up a few quarters in his enormous hand, straightened up, and then shuffled off down the hall. As he reached the end of the long corridor, he twisted his head around and yelled, "I'll be keepin' an eye on her, Crystal! No one assaults Red Andrews and gets away with it!"

"Oh, get a life, Wayne!" shouted Crystal. Christine and Julia chimed in, "Yeah, Wayne." Sarah noticed that their voices were not quite as loud or sure as Crystal's.

All of a sudden the frozen traffic sprang back to life, and Sarah found herself knocked against the wall next to Crystal and her friends.

"Hey, thanks," she muttered.

"No problem," said Crystal, smiling. "That big bully loves to harass people. Don't let him scare you."

"Who is he?"

"Wayne? Everyone calls him 'Red,' except us and the teachers. He's the varsity muscle-man . . ."

"And muscle-brain," added one of the other girls, chuckling.

"He's Springfield's hero," continued Crystal. "You know—football star, champion wrestler, baseball slugger. All-around jock . . . and stud."

The girls laughed at their own joke. Sarah smiled and began to relax for the first time that day. Starting a new school was harder than she had imagined. After fourteen years living in the same small suburban community, going to public school with the same kids, it was a shock being a stranger. She knew no one in her new neighborhood or synagogue or here at Springfield. Going to private school in the middle of a large unfamiliar city was both exhilarating and overwhelming. And what a way to begin her new life—colliding with Tarzan in front of the entire student body!

"What's your name?" asked Crystal.

"Sarah. I just moved here two weeks ago. My father got transferred."

"Welcome to the big city, Sarah."

Crystal shook her head, and Sarah found herself admiring the silky blond mane spilling over the tall girl's shoulders and down her back. "I'm Crystal. This is Christine and Julia."

Sarah nodded toward them and shifted uneasily on her feet. Now what? Should she ask them to help her find her first-period class? Would that make her seem stupid, or pushy? She shouldn't press her luck.

"Uh, gotta be going. The bell's gonna' ring any minute."

"Hey, relax. You've got plenty of time," Crystal reassured her. "Nobody takes schedules seriously the first day. What's your first class? We'll walk you there."

It was as easy as that. The rest of the day, Sarah was shepherded around like some visiting dignitary. At lunch, Crystal, Julia, and Christine invited her to sit with them in the cafeteria, filled her in on the hottest gossip, and then waltzed her around to meet their other friends. By the end of the day, Sarah felt lightheaded and happier than she had ever been. How stupid she had been to accuse her parents of ruining her life by moving away from the only home she'd ever known! Compared to these sophisticated city kids, her old friends—Deirdre, Diane, even Danny Green—seemed like hicks. Not that they weren't nice, but they lacked the sparkle and savvy of these new friends. Yes, this was the right place to be. She was finally about to begin living her life for real.

"Hey, Sarah," Crystal called to her from her locker several yards away. "You free Friday night?"

"Friday? No . . . I mean, I'm not sure. Maybe. I have to check. Why?"

"I'm having a pool party at my house. I'd like you to come."

Sarah felt the blood rush hotly into her face. Friday night! That was Shabbat dinner. Her favorite uncle, actually great-uncle Aaron, was coming for the weekend, and her parents had also invited a family from their new synagogue—they had a daughter Sarah's age—for dinner. They would never let her get out of the meal to go to a pool party. Well, they would have no choice. Sarah wouldn't give them any. She was an adult now. And this was a big city, not just some hick town where nobody had Friday night pool parties. Her parents had no right to make all the rules for her anymore.

"Come to think of it, Crystal, I *am* free," Sarah said emphatically, nodding her head. "What time?"

"Six. We'll swim first, then eat and hang out for a few hours. I want to introduce you to the gang. I think you'll like them. The address is 500 Stanton Lane, off Cedar and Harding. Just come around back and holler. Someone'll let you in."

"I'll be there!"

Sarah watched Crystal's slim form grow smaller until it disappeared through the double doors. She noticed that she was now alone in the long, brightly lit corridor.

Why had she done that? Why had she told Crystal that she could come before talking to her parents? What if they absolutely said no? Would she go anyway? And what if she didn't come? Would Crystal ever invite her to anything again?

For once, luck was with Sarah. When she got home from school that day, her mother told her that her great-uncle had called just hours before to cancel his trip. He was just not feeling up to the two-hour train ride. And the Gormans had canceled, too, because Mrs. Gorman's mother had died and they had to fly to California for the funeral.

Sarah tried to conceal her delight, but Mrs. Eisenberg saw right through her.

"I thought you liked Uncle Aaron, Sarah."

"Oh, I do, Mom! I love him. It's just that . . ."

"Oh, so it's the Gormans. Now don't give me that line about not liking to meet new kids at family meals. You and Vivie Gorman would have had plenty of time to get to know each other— away from us. You could have excused yourselves right after the main course and gone off by yourselves. At your age it's good for you to practice your interpersonal skills in a variety of settings."

Sarah groaned. Why did every social occasion have to turn into a therapy session!

"It's not that, Mom. It's just that I have other plans."

"What other plans? I thought you didn't know anyone here yet."

"I met some kids at school."

Mrs. Eisenberg beamed. "Why didn't you say so? Oh, Sarah, I'm thrilled! It's just what Dad and I were hoping would happen. When we visited Springfield, we saw so many kids who reminded us of you. We just knew you'd fit right in."

"Mom, you make it sound like I fell in love with somebody at first sight!" Sarah let out a whoosh of exasperation. Honestly, her mother lived on some other planet!

"OK, so who did you meet and what are your . . . plans?"

"I met this girl named Crystal and her two friends, Christine and Julia. They sort of acted like tour guides for me today."

"Are they Jewish?"

"What has that got to do with anything!"

Sarah dropped her heavy backpack on the kitchen floor and slumped down at the kitchen table. "I told you—I'm not marrying anyone!"

"I was just asking out of curiosity, Sarah."

Sarah smiled sheepishly. "Sorry, I guess I'm a little grumpy. I'd better have something to eat to fix that."

She walked over to the refrigerator and poked her head into the freezer. She reemerged with a quart container of Rocky Road ice cream. She sat back down at the table and began digging into the ice cream with great energy.

"So . . ."

"So what?"

"So, are you going to tell me about your plans?"

"Oh, yeah." Sarah licked her thumb and began spooning large gobs of ice cream into her mouth. "Crystal invited me to a pool party this Friday night at her house. And dinner and stuff."

Sarah looked up at her mother and noticed the familiar furrow in the center of her forehead. Uh-oh. That always spelled trouble, and a long lecture.

"That's Shabbat, Sarah."

"I know. But it's a once-in-a-lifetime chance, Mom! I'm starting a new school and the coolest girl in the whole school invites me to meet her crowd. It'll get me set for my whole high school career. And if I don't go, she'll be insulted and I'll be an outcast for four years!"

Mrs. Eisenberg raised her eyebrows. "Come on, Sarah, there will be other parties, believe me."

"But I won't invited to them! Can't we make an exception just this once, Mom? I promise not to accept again without talking it over with you first."

"You already said yes?"

Sarah gulped. Now she'd done it. It was bad enough that she was considering breaking the Sabbath to go to the party, but accepting the invitation without first consulting her parents would really irritate them.

But she was wrong this time.

"I really wish you hadn't done that, Sarah," her mother said, shaking her head. "Now you really will hurt the girl's feelings if you tell her you can't come. I'll have to talk it over with your father, but I think we should let you go this once. I assume the girl's parents will be home to chaperone?"

Sarah nodded, although she had no idea if it was true. She suspected that Crystal's parents were the sort not to meddle too much in their daughter's affairs.

"And I want you to promise me that you will talk such things over with us in the future. While you are living in our house, we have to insist that you play by our rules. When you're on your own . . ."

"I can make my own rules," finished Sarah. She had heard this speech at least a thousand times before. And she hated it. Many of her parents' rules weren't even theirs but were the rules of some old rabbis from a million years ago. But this was almost the twenty-first century. It was time for some of the rules to change!

"Thanks, Mom!"

"It's not definite, Sarah!" her mother shouted at Sarah's retreating back as she bounded up the stairs toward her room. "And it can't be a late . . ."

Sarah's door slammed before she could finish her sentence.

Crystal Hunter's house—a grand three-story mansion located in a fancy part of the city—looked like something right out of the movies. As Sarah and her father pulled up to the front door, Sarah noted that the long circular drive was parked up with sports cars. Quickly she jumped out of her father's car, slammed the door, and shooed the car away as if it were a bothersome fly. How embarrassing to be dropped off by your father—and in a dented mini-van, no less! At least no one was out in front to see her.

Following Crystal's instructions, she ran around to the back and yelled "Hello!" as loudly as she could.

A young woman wearing a black uniform with a white apron opened the wooden gate and let her in. "One of Miss Crystal's friends?"

"Umm," Sarah mumbled, her breath taken away by the view revealed behind the gate. Crystal's backyard was even more magnificent than the front. The built-in pool was surrounded by a wide concrete walk leading to a stone patio near the house. Off to one side was a little building painted in pastels, and a gazebo where several boys and girls sat huddled together, laughing. Flaring torches on long stems filled the backyard with warm yellow light. Rock music played softly in the background. Sarah could smell meat roasting somewhere nearby, and she heard the clink of ice in glasses. In the dim light, she could just make out a few small clusters of people around the yard, some sitting on lawn chairs, some standing. She guessed there were about twenty kids in all, more than she'd expected . . . and half were boys.

"Sarah! Over here!"

Sarah turned her head toward the pool and craned to see who had called her. It was Crystal, who had just surfaced from a dive and was shaking off water with a toss of her head.

"Glad you made it. Get into your suit right away and jump in. The water's great!"

Sarah started walking toward the house to change, but the maid pointed to the little pink-and-blue house off to the side. "You can change in there."

Seconds later, Sarah emerged from the cabana in her suit, a tight navy blue one-piece cut too low for her parents' taste but not low enough for anyone under thirty. She ran up to the edge of the pool, took a deep breath, and dove in, shocked and thrilled by the cold bite of the water. When she surfaced, she found herself staring into an unfamiliar face.

"Hi," said the girl. She had a rather pinched face, with the squinty eyes of someone who depends on glasses to see anything, a ridiculously small nose, and a mouth that never seemed to stop squirming. Her hair, slicked down by the water, looked like a potful of macaroni stuck together. Sarah couldn't imagine how someone like this had been invited to this party.

"My name is Cynthia Tinkler. You must be the new freshman."

Sarah smiled. Cynthia Tinkler. Perfect! A name to fit the face.

"My name's Sarah. Yeah, I'm new."

"I hope you like it at Springfield. I've been there since kindergarten."

Sarah tried to figure out a way to escape from Cynthia. She spotted Christine with a few others at the deep end. "Uh, see you around, Cynthia," she said, and started swimming toward the deep end before waiting for Cynthia's response.

"I see you met Cynthia," laughed Christine when Sarah got close to the others. "Quite something, isn't she? She's Springfield's secret weapon against all enemies."

The three others laughed. It was obvious that Cynthia was a favorite target of their jokes. Then why was she here? Surely she couldn't be part of Crystal's "gang."

As if reading her mind, Christine said, "We're going to have a little fun with Cynthia tonight, Sarah. In fact, you're going to be a key part of the fun."

Sarah's eyes widened with surprise. "Me?"

"It's one of Crystal's most brilliant ideas yet! While Cynthia's still in the pool, you sneak into the cabana and steal her clothes. You can hide them in the house somewhere. Then, when she goes to change, we tell her to toss us her wet suit and towel, and—guess what, no clothes! I can't wait to hear Cynthia's reaction!"

"I can't do that! I don't even know her."

"Even better. She'll never suspect you. It's just a joke, Sarah! We'll give her back her clothes after we've had a little fun."

Sarah gulped and looked back at Cynthia, swimming by herself in the middle of the pool. She was certainly a laughable person, but that didn't mean people could be cruel to her. How horrible to be invited to a party just so others could make fun of you!

"I don't think I want to do it," Sarah said softly.

"I think you should, Sarah," said Christine, smiling rather wickedly, Sarah thought. "Otherwise, Crystal's feelings will be hurt. She hates it when people spoil her great ideas. It's locker seven, by the way. In the cabana."

Realizing she was trapped, Sarah swam slowly to the ladder and pulled herself out of the water. She walked slowly toward the cabana and closed the door behind her. Inside locker seven was a neatly folded pile of clothes—plaid shorts, a white short-sleeved shirt, thongs, thick tortoise-shell glasses, white cotton underwear—and a bra! Sarah felt embarrassed touching these private things, but she didn't know what else to do. She wrapped the clothes in a towel, clutched the bundle to her chest, and closed the locker door. Out of curiosity she opened up a few of the other lockers—they were all empty. Clearly, this little joke had been well planned. Quickly she left the cabana and slipped into the house through the sliding glass doors.

It was dark inside. When her eyes adjusted, she looked around the family room and spotted a small couch against the wall. She ran over and stuffed the towel under one of the cushions. Then she ran back outside and dove into the pool. She was not surprised to find herself facing Cynthia when she surfaced.

"Quite some place, isn't it, Sarah? I never thought she'd ever invite me. I guess she's maturing, making room for other sorts of people. I may not be like her and her friends, but there's a lot to me beneath the surface."

Sarah nodded, glancing quickly around the pool for others, but they were alone.

"So, Sarah, do you have any hobbies?"

"Uh, you know, Cynthia, I'm hungry. Starving, in fact. I think I'll check out what there is to eat."

Again she fled Cynthia, going as far away from the cabana as she could. In the corner farthest from the house, she discovered a white wrought-iron bench under a small tree and sat down, suddenly shivering in the chilly September night. She fixed her gaze on the pool and waited.

Cynthia came out of the pool and walked over to the cabana. Sarah kept her eyes glued on the small, awkward body until it vanished into the small house. She looked around the backyard and saw that everyone else was staring at the cabana. Obviously, this was the featured entertainment of the evening.

Suddenly Crystal's voice rang out over the low music.

"Toss out your wet suit and towel, Cynthia. I'm throwing all the wet stuff into the dryer so it'll be dry when everyone's ready to leave."

Seconds later, a skinny arm emerged from behind the cabana door, dangling a wet bathing suit and white towel by its finger-tips. Quickly, Crystal ran up to the arm, snatched the wet garments from the hand, and ran off toward the house, holding her other hand over her mouth to stifle her laughter.

Silence fell over the yard. Even the music had been turned down until it was barely audible. Sarah realized she was holding her breath and let it out slowly.

"Hey, what's the big idea!" Cynthia's voice was squeaky and loud.

Now the yard exploded in gales of laughter. Sarah's stomach tightened into a knot.

"OK, some joke, you guys! Now that you've had your fun, give me back my clothes."

"Show us what you've got, Tinkler!" a male voice shouted. "I've heard it's not to be believed!"

More laughter, this time accompanied by whistles and catcalls.

"Come on, this isn't funny! I want my clothes! You'll pay for this!"

"Aw, just show us a little skin, Cynthia. Make our night!"

Sarah felt her cheeks burning. She was partly responsible for this horrible scene. Sure, they would have stolen Cynthia's clothes anyway, but there was no denying that she had agreed to this prank. She imagined what it would feel like if she were the one in the cabana now, naked and shivering, shamed in public, laughed at. But what could she do for Cynthia now?

"Come on, you guys, gimme back my clothes! Please, I'm begging you! At least give me back my glasses! How am I going to get home? Don't just leave me here! Please!"

She was crying now. The words came out in choppy pieces. No one replied this time. The joke was getting boring. First Christine, then a couple of others walked toward the house. In a few moments, they were all gone, leaving an empty pool, patio, and yard. Cynthia's whimperings continued for a few more minutes, then stopped.

Sarah stood up and ran toward the cabana. Then she stopped and spun on her heels, heading toward the house. Sliding back the glass door, she stepped into the dark house. When her eyes adjusted, she saw that the family room was empty. From upstairs drifted the sound of happy young voices and the tangy smells of roasted meat. Taking off her thongs and carrying them so as not to make any noise, Sarah ran to the couch, thrust her hand under the cushion, and grabbed the towel wrapped around Cynthia's clothes. She stepped back outside, slid the door shut behind her, and ran over to the cabana.

"Here, Cynthia, put these on—but don't tell *anyone* who gave them to you. If you do, you're dead!"

"Sarah? Is that you? I knew you weren't one of them. Hey, thanks. I'll do the same for you sometime."

"Forget it," Sarah mumbled. "Remember, not a word to anyone. Just make something up. Or just leave."

"I can't just leave. I live about three miles from here. I have to go inside and call my mom to come get me. What'll I say if I can't tell them it was you?"

But Sarah was already back in the house, joining the happy voices and smells.

"Hey, Crystal, look what the cat dragged in!"

Cynthia stood in the doorway to the vast living room, hands on her hips, her square jaw set in anger. Behind her thick glasses, her dark brown eyes looked enormous.

"So, are you going to tell us how you got your clothes back, Cynthia? Have you been giving the neighbors a thrill?"

Off to one side, Crystal stood near an immense aquarium, glowing soft blue, filled with brightly colored fish. She was surrounded by several young men, obviously admirers. Her blond hair was once again perfectly combed, framing her tanned relaxed face. On that face was a smile, but Sarah could see that she wasn't pleased.

"I wrapped a towel around myself and came in to look for my clothes. It doesn't take a Sherlock Holmes to unravel your juvenile crimes."

Mustering as much dignity as she could, Cynthia spun on her heels, marched toward the phone on the wall, and punched in her home number.

"Mother? I'd like you to come immediately to pick me up at the Hunters'. I think I've had my fill of this party. I'll be waiting out in front."

She slammed the receiver down and walked briskly toward the front door, not turning around. All this time, no one spoke or moved. As soon as the heavy front door closed behind her, Christine broke the silence.

"Well, Sarah, do I sense a traitor in our midst?"

She was staring straight at Sarah, glaring at her through narrow blue eyes. Sarah felt the knot tighten in her gut.

"You heard what Cynthia said, Christine. She found the clothes! I didn't tell her where they were!"

Which was all *technically* true. Sarah hadn't told Cynthia where she had hidden the clothes. And Cynthia had found them—at the end of Sarah's arm. She wasn't really lying; she was just leaving out some of the truth.

"Sarah, if what Christine says is true, this is pretty serious. We depend upon absolute loyalty from each other and to the gang. We can't have traitors among us."

"I swear I'm not a traitor! I want to be your friend, honest!"

Crystal walked over to Sarah and put one hand on her shoulder. "I know you do, Sarah. That's why I invited you to my party. It's just that so many people want to be my friend, and not all of them are the right sort of friend. I've learned to be careful."

Sarah didn't like the tone of Crystal's voice. Underneath the friendliness was a threat. It was obviously not a good idea to get on Crystal's wrong side.

"Umm . . . I've got to go," said Sarah, walking toward the phone. "My parents told me not to make it too late a night."

"Well, we wouldn't want to upset Mommy and Daddy, now would we?" purred Crystal. There it was again, that nasty edge to her voice. "Too bad my parents aren't even home tonight to check up on me. Maybe I should give *them* a curfew."

The laughter of the other kids hurt even more than Crystal's words. Sarah wanted to leave that instant, but she knew she had to call her father and wait for him to come. Luckily, he had nothing planned for tonight. He could be here in fifteen minutes.

"Wanna talk about it?" Mr. Eisenberg asked when he picked Sarah up in front of the Hunter mansion about twenty minutes later.

"There's nothing to talk about, Dad," Sarah snapped. "It was just a boring party so I decided to leave."

"Mom told me that you considered it a 'once-in-a-lifetime party' when you first told her about it."

"So I exaggerated. You know how teenagers are."

Mr. Eisenberg chuckled. "Suit yourself. Judging from the house and grounds, I would say that these aren't your sort of people, Sarah."

"What's with everyone, anyway!" Sarah burst out. "Why does everyone have to be classified into 'sorts' of people—geeks, rich kids, Jews? Why can't we just be people without labels?"

"So you do want to talk about it, eh?" Mr. Eisenberg's voice was gentle and a little teasing.

"I told you I didn't, Dad. Let's just drop it, OK?"

They rode the rest of the way in silence. Neither Alan nor Elaine Eisenberg was surprised to hear Sarah's bedroom door slam when she ran up to her room to bed.

2

Loyalty Test

Sarah was surprised to discover how quickly she could forgive and forget. For a few days after the incident at Crystal's party, she swore to herself that she would never speak to Crystal and her friends again. But her resolve didn't last long. How could it, when Crystal and the others went out of their way to win her back, admitting that they had been horribly cruel to Cynthia and pleading with Sarah to give them another chance? She was flattered by their attention—and still eager for their friendship. And they were still the only friends she had.

And boy, did she need friends! The academic part of high school was turning out to be tougher than she had thought it would be. As much as she enjoyed some of the classes, especially her English class, where they were studying the poetry of Emily Dickinson, which she loved, the homework was unbelievable. During the first week of school she had averaged two hours a night, and the teachers were warning them that it would only get heavier when they started their term projects. If it weren't for the promising social life, she would have tried to persuade her parents to transfer her to Central High, the city's best public high school. It couldn't possibly be as hard as Springfield. But if she transferred she would never meet people like Crystal Hunter.

"Hey, Sarah!" shouted a familiar voice.

She looked up from her locker to see Crystal walking toward her—arm in arm with Wayne Andrews!

"Wanna come to the Apple Core with Red and me?"

Wayne smiled, scattering clouds of freckles over his pocked cheeks. He no longer seemed the terrifying enemy of that first day, but struck Sarah as just a big dopey-looking guy with over-sized hands and feet. Like a St. Bernard puppy, she decided. It might even be fun to have him as a friend.

"Yeah, how about it, Sarah?" said Wayne, grabbing her by the elbow. "I'll give you girls a ride."

Sarah bit her lip and looked down at her feet. What should I do, she thought. It's Friday afternoon, only one week after the fiasco at the pool party. I promised Mom and Dad that I would be home early today to help them prepare for Shabbat dinner. Uncle Aaron's coming, and so are Mr. Gorman and Vivie. They'll kill me if I break my promise.

"Uh . . . can I take a rain check, Way . . . Red? I can't make it today."

"Oh, come on, Sarah," pleaded Crystal. "Friday afternoon's the best time to be at the Apple Core. Tony gives two-for-one's on the doughnuts."

"I promised to help with dinner."

"So you'll help tomorrow night instead."

"Well . . . tonight's kind of special."

"Birthday or somethin'?" asked Wayne.

Sarah didn't understand why she just didn't tell them the truth? Why was she beating around the bush like this? Why was she embarrassed to say that it was because of Shabbat?

"My parents are pretty strict about our being together for this meal. You see, it's . . . our Sabbath meal. It's the fanciest meal of the week."

There—she'd said it!

She was relieved to see Wayne's reaction—or rather, nonreaction. He looked down at his dirty fingernails, then at his watch. He shifted from one foot to the other, restless and bored. Obviously, all he was thinking about was getting to the Apple Core as soon as possible.

But that wasn't the case with Crystal. She was staring at Sarah now, her mouth hanging open like a Venus flytrap. Sarah definitely did not like the look in her cold blue eyes.

"Sabbath?" Crystal almost spit out the word. "Don't tell me you're Jewish?"

"As a matter of fact, I am. I thought you knew, Crystal. It's no big deal."

"Well, are we goin' or not?" interrupted Wayne. "I'll never get a parking space if we don't get there soon."

Sarah shook her head. "Not today. Maybe Monday, OK?"

"Sure, Sarah. Monday."

Wayne smiled at her and began tugging at Crystal's elbow. Impatiently, Crystal shook him off and turned to face Sarah.

"Jewish, eh? Why didn't you tell us?"

Sarah didn't know what to say. She hadn't purposely kept her Jewishness a secret. It just hadn't come up. And what was the big deal anyway? What difference did it make?

"Oh, forget it," snapped Crystal, grabbing Wayne's arm and tugging him toward the front doors of the building. "Come on, Red, I want to get there before all the glazed doughnuts are gone."

Sarah watched them head down the hallway. Even after they had disappeared through the doors, she kept staring in that direction. What had just happened? Why did she feel so funny? Why were her feelings suddenly so mixed up? Why did she feel embarrassed and angry and disappointed and jealous, all at the same time? What a hopeless tangle! And who could help her figure it out?

The Apple Core was only four blocks from Springfield School. An easy walk, but no one walked there from school unless it was absolutely necessary. Kids with cars drove; those without, hitched rides. In nice weather like today, most of the kids hung out around the sidewalk tables, checking out the cars, seeing who came with whom, and more important, especially on Fridays, who left with whom.

On this Friday afternoon in mid-September, the tables were crowded with Springfield kids. By the time Crystal and Red arrived, every plastic chair was taken, as was every car hood and stoop in the vicinity. Their arrival was greeted with loud hello's and cheers. Clearly, Crystal was the queen of this small kingdom, and if Wayne wasn't exactly the king, he was certainly respected. Magically, two chairs suddenly became vacant at the table nearest to the front door of the restaurant as Crystal and

Wayne threaded through the crowd. Soon Tony himself appeared, carrying two menus and two tall glasses of ice water.

"Crystal! Red! Glad to see ya! What'll ya have?"

"How 'bout a dozen doughnuts, Tony, mixed? Usual deal?"

"Of course, Red." He bent over toward Crystal. "How 'bout you, babe?"

"Two white glazed ones for me, Tony. Hold the calories."

Tony laughed and set the water glasses down. "Sure thing, babe. I've saved the best for you. Not a calorie between 'em. How about something to drink?"

"The usual, Tony. Small diet for Crystal here and a large root beer for me."

Tony disappeared into the restaurant and came back quickly with the order. Then he went back inside, where loud music boomed in the semi-darkness.

"Hey, Christine, Julia!" Crystal shouted to the two girls sitting with several others on the cement steps next door. "Come here. I have something interesting to tell you."

Christine and Julia hurried over. With a wave of her hand, Crystal cleared everyone else from the table, leaving several empty chairs for her friends. Even Wayne, seeing that he was no longer wanted, shuffled off to take the girls' place among the small knot of young people hanging out at the nearby stoop.

"OK, Crystal," said Julia, leaning forward and lowering her voice, "What's up?"

"I know you've both been after me to drop the idea of testing Sarah's loyalty after what happened last week. You seem to feel it's not necessary anymore."

"I thought you agreed with us," said Christine. "Sarah's really OK. We all think so."

"I'm not so sure, Christine," Crystal said, biting down on her words to let her friend know that she was upset. "I've just learned that our 'OK' friend has a secret."

Julia and Christine bent forward eagerly.

"Ready for this? She's Jewish!" Crystal announced triumphantly.

"Is that all? So what?" asked Julia. "Why is that such a secret?"

Crystal looked miffed. "So what? She didn't even tell us!" She sat back and folded her sleek arms over her chest, leaning back in her chair. "So tell me, Ms. Genius—do we have any other Jews in our gang?"

Julia frowned. "Well, come to think of it, I guess not. But I don't think it's that way on purpose."

"Don't be such a jerk, Julia!" snapped Crystal. "Of course, it's on purpose. I don't like that sort in my circle of friends. My dad's told me all about them. They're totally obsessed with money, and they think they're better than everyone else. And they're incredibly cliquish."

"Hey, sounds like us!" joked Julia. Christine laughed. Crystal did not. The other two stopped laughing as soon as they saw their friend's scowl.

"So what are you getting at, Crystal?" asked Christine.

"Well, I'm willing to give Sarah the benefit of the doubt. Maybe she's different than the rest of them. I say we find out just how loyal she is to us—and how loyal she is to her own kind."

Christine looked at Julia, then at Crystal. "Is what you're planning legal, Crystal? There are laws about these things, you know. I don't want to get into any trouble."

Crystal laughed. "Relax, Christine. It's just a little honest fun. Like we had with Cynthia—only more so."

She laughed loudly, and the other two girls joined in. Soon they were trading Cynthia imitations, making so much noise that Tony came outside to see what was going on. He smiled to see them laughing with such enthusiasm. Such nice young people! It made him feel young just being around them.

Dominique Rosenblatt loved being a cub reporter on the *Springfield Gazette*. She loved hanging around the newsroom with the juniors and seniors, hearing about the news before the rest of the Springfield students, eavesdropping on high-level decisions by the senior editors and their faculty advisor, Dr. Meyers. One of her favorite tasks was coming up with headlines for the news articles. After the news editor gave her the space count, she would have to find just the right words to fit into that number of spaces. She loved solving puzzles like this, and even the seniors on the newspaper staff told her that she was one of the best headline writers they'd ever had. She promised herself that when she became senior news editor in three years, she would still do some headlines—just for the fun of it.

Today she was struggling with a particularly hard assignment: coming up with a headline for an article about school cliques. Dominique didn't like the article at all. The reporter, Naomi Levy, a nerdy junior, actually named names in the article. She had especially targeted Crystal Hunter and her gang, calling them snobby and petty. How horrible for Crystal! Could she help the fact that she was rich and popular? Obviously Naomi was just jealous. If she were one of Crystal's gang, she wouldn't feel this way.

Dominique knew how she felt, though. She herself had been jealous of Crystal ever since they'd started Springfield together ten years ago. Of course, when Dominique was younger she couldn't admit it, but she now saw that she had always wanted to be Crystal's friend. Her mother had told her that they didn't travel in the same circles so she could just forget about breaking into that crowd. But Dominique had never stopped hoping.

And now she finally had her chance. Recently her father had been appointed director of Midtown Healthcare Company. He was making so much money that the Rosenblatts had been able to buy *two* new cars and a sailboat within the last three months. They now were traveling in the same circles as the Hunters. It was time for Crystal to invite her in.

A knock on the newsroom door broke into her train of thought. She looked up to see a smiling face looking at her through the little window. Crystal Hunter! Had the other girl been reading her thoughts? Was this the moment Dominique had been dreaming about all these years? Was Crystal coming to welcome her into the inner circle right now?

She sprang up from her chair and ran to open the door. Crystal walked right by her, swinging her head from side to side as if searching for something.

"Hi, Crystal! Funny you should come here today. I was just thinking about you."

Crystal's smile widened, her eyes still scanning the scattered papers on the large wooden table.

"Ummm," she replied, absent-mindedly.

Dominique rushed on, excited. "Yeah, I was thinking about you and me, about how much we have in common."

Crystal turned and locked her gaze on Dominique, frightening her with the intensity of her stare. "In common, huh? What could the two of us possibly have in common?"

Dominique began to stutter, something that always happened when she became nervous. "W . . . w . . . well, we're both rich, for one thing!"

That hadn't come out right, thought Dominique. How uncool could I be! What a dumb thing to say. But maybe I can repair the damage.

"What I mean is that we both have an appreciation for the finer things. We're different from ordinary people, you and I, we're . . . s . . . s . . . special."

Crystal laughed. "Oh, come off it, Rosenblatt! Just because your dad's got money now doesn't make you an aristocrat!"

Dominique sat down, stunned. This wasn't at all what she had imagined would happen. She was screwing it up totally! Maybe her mother was right about traveling in the same circles. Well, she would give it one last shot before giving up.

"I know you're not like it says in the article, Crystal. I've watched you all these years. You're really a very nice person."

"So there *is* an article about me!" shouted Crystal, craning her neck toward the littered table. "Where is it?"

Dominique thought quickly. It was against newspaper policy to show anyone articles before publication. Dr. Meyers felt very strongly about censorship and had vowed to protect her reporters from public pressure. If Dominique showed Crystal the article, she might get suspended from the paper.

On the other hand, was it fair for Crystal *not* to see the article, since it was about her? Her reputation was on the line. She had a right to know what was coming. If she promised not to tell anyone . . .

"I can't really show you the article, Crystal," Dominique said, slowly moving toward the place at the table where the article lay. "It's against our rules. But I can tell you that you are mentioned. And not in the nicest words."

"I know you're my friend, Dominique," purred Crystal, coming closer. "You know what it'll do to me if that article comes out. I would be really grateful if it didn't."

Dominique shook her head. "I can't do it, Crystal. I'm sorry, but I don't make decisions about what does and doesn't go into the paper. I just write the headlines and help with the layout."

"But I bet you have influence," said Crystal. "I bet you could use your influence to change the *tone* of the article. Don't you think so?"

Dominique again shook her head. "Sorry, Crystal, I can't do it. Our writers have complete editorial freedom."

"Who's the writer, then?" asked Crystal. Her voice had become gruff and angry. "Maybe I can talk to him."

"Naomi Levy."

"Levy! I should have known! You Jews, you're all in this together!" Crystal exploded. "You think you can go around criticizing anyone you want, pretending you're better than everyone else. Well, let me tell you something, Rosenblatt—you don't own the world. And you sure don't own me!"

Crystal spun on her heels and stormed out of the tiny room, slamming the door behind her. Dominique stood near her chair, stunned and speechless.

What was Crystal talking about? Who ever said Jews owned the world? And why did Crystal lump her together with other Jews? She didn't even consider herself really Jewish. Sure, she had a Jewish name and lit Hanukkah candles and liked Jewish food, but she also loved Christmas trees, lobster tails, and Gregorian chants. She didn't even have a single Jewish friend! Being Jewish was just a fact about her, like being American or female or short. It certainly didn't define her identity.

Biting down on the end of her pencil, Dominique bent over the paper in front of her and stared at the headlines she had thought of so far:

CLIQUES DON'T CLICK AT SPRINGFIELD
WHO'S LEFT OUT BY IN-CROWD AND WHY
NO ROOM AT THE INN —IF YOU'RE OUT

She drew a giant X through all three, then crumpled up the paper into a tight wad and tossed it into the metal can in the corner. Taking a clean sheet, she wrote:

THE CLIQUE MYSTIQUE: A TRUE STORY

Ha! she thought to herself. Some true story! As if anyone really understands how these things work! One thing's for certain—I sure as hell don't.

Sarah first heard about the incidents involving Dominique Rosenblatt at a freshman assembly at the end of September. The principal, Mr. Johnson, gave them a short lecture about prejudice, referring to some "regrettable episodes in our own school community." When someone asked him to explain, he mentioned that certain antisemitic remarks had been made to a freshman "who shall remain nameless." This same student had also received crank calls in a fake Yiddish accent and had found antisemitic graffiti spray-painted on her locker. Mr. Johnson warned that such behavior would not be tolerated at Springfield.

As they were leaving the auditorium, Sarah overheard two of her classmates naming Dominique Rosenblatt as the student under attack. She was so surprised that she stopped dead in her tracks.

Sarah knew who Dominique was. Springfield's classes were so small that she had been able to learn everyone's name by the second week of school. Sarah had not been interested in getting to know Dominique better. The girl had a big mouth, and was always putting other kids down. And she was always bragging about how rich she was—not like Crystal and her friends, who were so cool about their wealth.

Now that Sarah thought about it, she realized that Dominique had been acting different over the past week. She had been unusually quiet, even kind of depressed. And her eyes were frequently red. Sarah had assumed that she had a bad allergy. Maybe she should seek her out at lunch today, give her a little support after all she'd been going through.

But when Sarah got to the cafeteria at fifth period, Dominique wasn't there. She wasn't in the cafeteria the next day, either, or the next. In class, Dominique kept to herself, running out of the room as soon as the bell rang, hardly ever looking up or talking to anyone. Sarah decided to find out why.

Christine and Julia said they knew nothing about it. But Crystal smiled when Sarah asked her about Dominique.

"Oh, it's awful, isn't it? A real shame. I've heard how high-strung Jews can be, but she'll need to grow a thicker skin if she wants to get along in the world."

"Do you know anything about this, Crystal?" asked Sarah, feeling a flush of anger warm her cheeks.

"Why do you think I know any more than you do?"

"Are you behind these antisemitic attacks on her?"

Crystal laughed. "Really, Sarah, is that any way for one friend to talk to another? I thought we were on the same team."

Sarah felt confused. Was Crystal mixed up in this or not? Why wouldn't she answer Sarah's questions? There was something going on here that Sarah didn't understand.

She tried again. "OK, Crystal, if we're on the same team, I say we try to find out who's behind these attacks and stop them."

Crystal glared at her. "Oh, don't be such a goody two-shoes, Sarah! It's bad enough that Johnson is making a federal case out of it. Don't you, too! Remember the rhyme from nursery school: 'Sticks and stones will break my bones, but words will never hurt me'? Well, I think it's good for Dominique Rosenblatt to be reminded of who she is. She thinks she can just dispose of her Jewishness like old sunburn!"

Sarah's mouth dropped open. So, Crystal *was* behind it! Although Sarah had read about antisemitism in books and had heard her parents talking about it, she had never before encountered it personally. In fact, she and her classmates in confirmation class had recently tried to convince Rabbi Axelrod that antisemitism didn't exist here in America. The rabbi had told them that they were naive.

Maybe the rabbi's right, thought Sarah. How else can I understand what Crystal said except as antisemitic propaganda? Or maybe she just doesn't realize what she's saying. Maybe she's just repeating stuff she heard at home. That's really what prejudice is, isn't it—ignorance, not evil. Crystal's not really a bad person, just a product of an ignorant family. Or, Sarah said to herself, am I being naive?

"Let me ask you something, Sarah," Crystal broke into her thoughts. "Remember my pool party back at the beginning of the school year."

Sarah nodded. How could she ever forget!

"Remember you swore at the time that you were not a traitor to our group?"

Again Sarah nodded.

"Well, how about proving it?"

Sarah felt sweat break out on the back of her neck and on her palms. What did Crystal have in mind? It was sure to be nasty. As much as she liked having so many new friends, there were some things about them that she hated—most of all, their idea of what was funny. It usually involved making someone else miserable.

"What do you want me to do, Crystal?"

"Nothing much. We're just going to have a little fun . . ."

"Meaning . . . ?"

"Spray-painting a design on Dominique's locker."

"What kind of design?"

"An ancient peace symbol." Crystal hesitated. "A swastika."

Sarah fell back as if she had been slapped by an invisible hand. A swastika! The symbol of the Nazis. No Jew could ever look at that image without being filled with pain and anger. How could Crystal even suggest that Sarah paint a swastika on another

Jew's locker? Was she serious? Was this another one of her sick jokes?

"I can't!" Sarah blurted out. "You couldn't pay me enough to make me do it."

"What about your loyalty, Sarah? A good team player does whatever her captain asks of her. Don't you want to stay on the team?"

"Not if I have to do things like that!" Sarah looked down to find that her hands had turned into fists. She could feel her legs shaking beneath her.

"Why don't you think about it for a day or two," suggested Crystal in a sweet voice. "I wouldn't want you to make any rash decisions that you'll live to regret."

That night, as Sarah lay in bed staring up into the blackness, she scolded herself for not telling Crystal off right then. How could she even consider remaining Crystal's friend after what she had asked Sarah to do? She never wanted to talk to Crystal again! But was that enough? Could she stop Crystal from expressing her hatred? Could she change her so that she no longer wanted to hate? And who could help her fight this thing that felt so much bigger than one person?

When she woke up, Sarah knew who she would go to—Dr. Meyers. Besides being the newspaper advisor, Dr. Meyers was one of the ninth-grade advisors, Sarah's advisor. And she was also a Jew.

As soon as Sarah shared her secret with Dr. Meyers, she felt a great weight lift from her shoulders. Dr. Meyers listened intently, then asked Sarah how she felt about what had happened. Sarah was shocked to find herself crying as she talked about her conversation with Crystal. She quickly choked back the tears.

"What can we do, Dr. Meyers? How can we stop Crystal and her gang from hurting more people?"

"The best weapon against ignorance, Sarah, is knowledge. The truth. Someone like Crystal Hunter hasn't had the kind of education you or I have had. I'm speaking about your other education, Sarah—as a Jew. Unfortunately, we Jews have become experts in suffering. We've had no choice. Our earliest memories include Bible stories about our people's slavery in Egypt, about wanderings in the desert, about destruction and exile. We teach our children about how hard it is to be Jewish. Each year at the Seder we remember that it could have been otherwise. And we keep reminding ourselves to look out for others less fortunate since we know what it's like to be strangers and victims of hatred."

Sarah was growing impatient from Dr. Meyers' lecture. "But what can we do *now*, Dr. Meyers?"

"Why don't you leave that to me, Sarah. I'll see about arranging a special program on this subject. Maybe some honest sharing of thoughts and feelings will bring things out into the open where we can deal with them." She smiled. "And don't worry, Sarah, your secret's safe with me. No one will ever know you spoke with me about this. I promise."

Despite Dr. Meyers's promise, Sarah left her office feeling nervous. Before heading back to her locker, she poked her head out the door and looked up and down the empty corridor before dashing out. She didn't stop running until she reached her locker and stuck her head inside. If Crystal were to find out . . .

One week later, the entire ninth grade class filed into the auditorium to watch the movie *Schindler's List*. Sarah had already seen the film twice, once with her parents and once at synagogue, but she was surprised to learn that most of her fellow students hadn't ever seen it—nor did they especially want to. Before the lights went out, she heard plenty of grumbling about "depressing" and "boring" movies.

But when the film was over and the lights came back on, there was absolute silence in the auditorium. Even after they were divided into small groups and sent to different rooms for group discussions, almost no one said a word. Sarah was not surprised to find herself in a group with Dominique Rosenblatt and Crystal Hunter. Nor was she surprised to find that Dr. Meyers was their discussion leader.

"So, what would you have done if you had been Oskar Schindler?" Dr. Meyers asked them after they had pulled their ten chairs into a tight circle.

No one said a word. Sarah looked around. It was impossible to read the faces of her fellow students. Everyone was looking down at the floor. She doubted whether her own face revealed much about her feelings.

"Well, if no one's going to begin, I might as well!" Crystal suddenly blurted out. "I say that the Jews got what they deserved. If it had been me, I wouldn't have risked my neck to save them. They should have left Germany when they had the chance. They obviously weren't wanted."

"How can you say that, Crystal?" shouted one boy sitting across from her in the circle. "Didn't you see what that Nazi commander was like! Don't blame the Jews for what happened to them. It wasn't their fault!"

"I can't believe you said that, Crystal!" another boy jumped in. "I think Schindler was a hero for what he did!"

"Yeah, a hero!"

"What are you, Hunter, a Nazi or something?"

One by one, the others argued with and criticized Crystal Hunter. All except Sarah and Dominique. They both sat quietly in their chairs, watching their non-Jewish classmates stand up for Schindler and the Jews. No one seemed to notice their silence or the sympathetic glances they occasionally exchanged with each other. By the time the bell rang twenty minutes later, Crystal Hunter was looking red-faced and defeated. Although she hadn't openly admitted she was wrong, she no longer sounded at all sure of herself. She was even stuttering a bit, which brought a smile to Dominique's lips.

As she was leaving the room, Sarah found Dominique standing outside in the hall, apparently waiting for her.

"How about some lunch?" she asked a bit hesitantly.

"Sure!" answered Sarah, smiling warmly.

"You know, Sarah," Dominique said as the two walked toward the cafeteria together, "that was the first time I actually felt really Jewish. Even when all this antisemitic stuff was happening to me, I felt like it was all some sort of horrible mistake. They were going after the wrong person. But today I felt connected in a way I never have before. How about you?"

"I guess I've felt connected all my life," said Sarah. "Until I started Springfield, that is. As soon as I met Crystal Hunter, I wanted to be just like her and her friends. I no longer wanted to be who I was. I felt like being Jewish was an embarrassment. I didn't want to follow all those old-fashioned rules that my parents made me follow all my life."

"I'm glad we had this program today, aren't you?" asked Dominique. "I was amazed that all these non-Jewish kids could feel this way about Jews. You know, I was beginning to think I'd have to transfer to a different school because of the antisemitic stuff here. But I can see that Crystal is really in a minority. Everybody else is on our side."

Sarah smiled. If she only knew who was responsible for the program. But maybe it's better that she didn't know. Let her think it was the school's idea. Let her be grateful for the Oskar Schindlers in the world as well as for the Sarah Eisenbergs. We *are* all on the same side. It's only Crystal and people like her who are not—despite what she thinks.

Just then, Sarah's nose picked up a familiar smell. "Pizza! And garlic bread!"

And before Dominique knew what was happening, Sarah was ten yards ahead of her, her shoulder-length brown hair flying in her wake.

3

A Date to Remember

Are you sure they know what they're getting into?" asked Mr. Eisenberg as he helped Sarah set the long dining room table. With all three leaves in, the table stretched from one end of the room to the other. Sarah counted out ten cloth napkins and began laying them on the left side of each plate. Then she headed for the kitchen.

When she returned with both fists full of silverware, Mr. Eisenberg laughed. "Sorry, I forgot to remind you, Sarah. We're using the sterling tonight. Only the best for Rosh Hashanah."

Ordinarily, Sarah would have been annoyed by all this fuss, but she wasn't tonight. The Rosenblatts were used to such fanciness. Sarah had eaten at their house just once, but that had been enough. Even though it had been a Wednesday night, they had used cloth napkins and a tablecloth. And they had served wine in gorgeous cut-glass decanters. Anyway, given how strange tonight's meal was going to be for them, with all this religious stuff, it was best that they feel at home as much as possible.

Suddenly, Sarah and her father heard a loud crash from the second floor. Mrs. Eisenberg came running out of the kitchen, wiping her hands on her apron and groaning. As she bolted up the stairs, Sarah and her dad looked at each other and silently mouthed, "Mikey!"

Mikey was Sarah's eight-year-old brother, who had joined the family two years before. When the Eisenbergs had decided to adopt a Down's syndrome child, Sarah had first been intrigued by, then nervous about, the idea. Of course, she loved Mikey—in fact, she had loved her smiley, pudgy new brother from the first minute she had met him, but he certainly had changed the family's style of doing things. Sometimes she wondered whether her parents regretted their decision, but she had never had the nerve to ask them.

Mrs. Eisenberg came down the stairs carrying a large green ceramic lamp with both hands. Sarah could see the wide crack dividing the lamp into two unequal pieces. It was one of the bedside lamps from her parents' bedroom.

"Well, so much for the matching pair," said Mrs. Eisenberg glumly. "Mikey kicked it while he was watching TV on our bed. Of course, he's sorry."

That was certainly a familiar line. Mikey was always sorry. At least he was when he was able to understand that he'd done something wrong. Most of the time, though, he seemed unaware of the role he played in all the small—and sometimes large—disasters that followed in his wake. But how could he be? He only had the mind of a three-year-old.

"You know, Elaine, I've been meaning to tell you all these years." Mr. Eisenberg was smiling broadly. Sarah thought he was especially handsome when he smiled like that. "I never did like those lamps. We only took them because my parents were going to give them away to Mrs. Harris next door. I think this is a perfect opportunity to replace *both* of them."

The three of them laughed. One of the things that had happened since Mikey had come was that Sarah was often included in such adult conversations. She was like a third parent to Mikey, and her parents treated her as one. That meant more responsibility, too, but she didn't mind. Most of the time.

"OK, Sarah, since this is largely your party, why don't you help me decide which desserts to serve tonight and which to save for tomorrow night. You know Dominique's tastes better than I do."

Sarah followed her mother into the kitchen and stared hungrily at the tantalizing array of desserts on the counter. Apple pie, pecan pie, candied crab apples, taiglach, halavah, brownies (Sarah had made those). How could she possibly decide what *not* to eat tonight?

"And don't forget, there's fresh fruit and sorbet in the fridge," her mother added, laughing as Sarah's tongue poked out of her mouth.

"This is torture, Mom!"

"Whatever we don't serve tonight, we'll have tomorrow night. It's the Rosenblatts who will miss out, not you."

"OK, then let's have the pies and . . . fruit and sorbet tonight. That won't be too strange for them."

Mrs. Eisenberg cocked her head to one side. "How do you know they wouldn't prefer delicacies like taiglach and halavah? For all we know, Dr. and Mrs. Rosenblatt might have grown up on such strange stuff."

Sarah snorted impatiently. "Give me a break, Mom! The Rosenblatts are as American as they come. They've never even heard of taiglach or halavah, let alone tasted it. I don't even know if they've even heard of Rosh Hashanah."

"So why did you invite them?"

How could she explain it to her mother? Now that she and Dominique had become best friends, she wanted to share her world with her. Maybe if Dominique saw the way her family celebrated Jewish holidays and Shabbat, she might understand Sarah better. Hey, she might even want to start doing some of this stuff herself. And then Sarah wouldn't feel like such an oddball at Springfield, where no one else seemed to be religious. But she couldn't say all that to her mother!

"They're Jewish, aren't they?" Sarah burst out. "Do I need another reason?"

"OK, OK, I was just curious."

Mrs. Eisenberg walked over to the stove and lifted the lid off one of the big aluminum pots. She stirred it with a long wooden spoon, then brought the spoon to her lips and sipped.

"Perfect," she sighed. "Not too salty this time." She spoke to Sarah without turning around. "Is matzah ball soup too strange for your guests—or can they cope?"

"Very funny, Mom," snorted Sarah. "Matzah ball soup is American now. Like bagels and lox." She walked to the threshold between the dining room and kitchen, then turned around. "I'm going to take a shower and change for dinner. Do you want me to get Mikey ready?"

"Thanks, sweetheart. I could use the help. Try to get him to wear the new light blue button-down shirt I bought him. He looks so nice in it. But don't insist if he puts up a fight."

An hour later Sarah came down, leading Mikey by the hand. Mikey did look nice in his new shirt. With his soft brown hair neatly combed, and his face scrubbed, he almost looked normal, except for the eyes, and the tongue that kept thrusting out from between his lips.

"Don't you look nice, Mikey!" said Uncle Aaron, who had arrived in the meantime and was sitting as usual in the rocking chair in one corner of the living room, chatting with Mr. Eisenberg. "I don't know if I've ever seen you looking more handsome! Come give your favorite great-uncle a big hug and kiss!"

Beaming from ear to ear, Mikey ran toward Uncle Aaron and threw himself into his outstretched arms, burying his head in the old man's chest. Uncle Aaron hugged him close and planted a loud kiss on top of his head, then smoothed down Mikey's hair with one bony hand. Mikey lifted up his face and gave his great-uncle a loud, wet kiss on the cheek.

"That's my boy!" shouted Uncle Aaron. "Now tell me what you've been up to."

Mikey screwed up his face with intense concentration and began to form his words with obvious effort. "I go to school on a bus. I made a butterfly today. Want to see?"

Without waiting for his answer, Mikey ran off to the kitchen and came back grasping a large paper butterfly. The construction-paper creature was covered with wild crayon marks in all colors. At the bottom of one wing was the letter M in bold black strokes.

"Wonderful, Mikey! Beautiful!"

Then Uncle Aaron noticed Sarah standing quietly in the hallway. He winked at her.

"Nu, Sarah, so how's my favorite grandniece? How's life in the big city? Your father tells me that you're buried neck-deep in homework these days."

"It's awful, Uncle Aaron! They think we have no life outside of school. And every teacher thinks he or she's the only one who gives homework. I'll never make it through the year!"

Uncle Aaron smiled and clucked his tongue. "Sure you will, Sarah. You're a smart cookie. You'll figure out how to survive—and even have a little time left over for TV and for those cockamamie CD's of yours."

Sarah giggled. She loved Uncle Aaron's weird vocabulary, a mixture of Yiddish, old-fashioned English, and God knows what else. Every Rosh Hashanah when she said the prayer "Who shall live and who shall die," she prayed that Uncle Aaron would be inscribed in the Book of Life for at least one more year. She would miss him so much when he was gone. Even more than she missed Grandma since her death a year ago.

"What else can you tell me about—besides the mountain of homework? Make any new friends?"

"As a matter of fact, I have. Dominique Rosenblatt. You'll meet her tonight."

"Dominique Rosenblatt? What kind of a name is that? Only in America!"

"She's very nice, Uncle Aaron. You'll see when you meet her. She's very sophisticated. Her whole family is."

As if on cue, the doorbell rang and Mikey ran to open the door. It was the Rosenblatts, each carrying a package and sporting a broad smile. Mikey jumped up and down wildly, clapping his hands.

"Presents! Presents!" he shouted.

Sarah ran to the door and opened it wide to admit the Rosenblatt clan. Mrs. Rosenblatt walked in first, thrusting out an enormous bouquet of flowers. Sarah grasped the green paper wrapper surrounding the stems and headed toward the kitchen to get a vase. Mr. Eisenberg stepped into the hallway and took the bottle of wine from Dr. Rosenblatt's left hand, shaking his right hand and introducing himself. He also shook Mrs. Rosenblatt's hand and ushered them both into the living room. It was a warm night, so they were not wearing coats, although Mrs. Rosenblatt had a fur stole of some kind around her shoulders.

After their parents had gone into the living room, Dominique stepped into the front hall, followed by her younger sister and brother. Imitating her parents, she held out a small package toward Sarah and said, "Dinner mints."

Sarah took the package and thanked her, noticing to her regret that the package read "milk chocolate." They were having brisket tonight, so she would have to figure out how to tell the Rosenblatts why they weren't serving their mints for dessert. Sarah led her friend into the living room to join the others.

The two younger Rosenblatt children still stood awkwardly in the hallway, looking around as if lost. Mikey came up to them and pointed to the small boxes in their hands.

"For me?"

The boy, about Mikey's age although taller, nodded and handed Mikey the rectangular box. Mikey grabbed it and tore off the paper to reveal a brightly colored box with various geometric shapes displayed on the cover. Eagerly Mikey opened the flap and poured out the contents. A small booklet fell to the floor, followed by dozens of oddly shaped pieces of colored paper which fluttered slowly to the shiny wooden floor. Mikey held the empty box up to one eye and peered inside.

"Where is the present?" he asked, disappointed.

The boy pointed to the mess of paper on the floor.

"It's origami, Mikey. You can make all kinds of things out of the shapes. You just have to follow the instructions."

Mikey stared at him in bewilderment. "Where's the present?" he repeated.

Mrs. Eisenberg came to the rescue. "We'll do it together, Mikey. I'll make all sorts of toys for you to play with and hang from your ceiling."

She gently took him by the hand and led him into the living room, placing a large cookie in one hand as she sat him on the couch next to his father. He took a bite of the cookie and settled into the soft cushion, humming quietly to himself.

"Who gets my box?" asked a small voice from the hall.

Mrs. Rosenblatt sprang up, laughing. "Oh, Nicole, I'm so sorry! We almost forgot about you. Come give your box to our hostess, dear."

The little girl, whose plump form and wild blond curls reminded Sarah of a cartoon character, walked up to Mrs. Eisenberg and held out her box, somewhat larger and more oblong than her brother's.

"This is for you, for having us," she said very seriously.

"Why, thank you, Nicole," said Mrs. Eisenberg, copying the little girl's serious tone, but with a smile.

She opened it slowly, exclaiming loudly when she saw what it was.

"I can't accept this! It's Waterford crystal!"

She held up the delicate bud vase for all to see.

"It's nothing," said Mrs. Rosenblatt, clearly pleased by Mrs. Eisenberg's excited reaction. "Just a little something I picked up. Please, you'll hurt my feelings if you won't accept it."

Mrs. Eisenberg glanced over at her husband, who nodded slightly. "OK, but I must insist that you not bring such exp . . . so many gifts next time. It really isn't necessary."

"Janice and I are so pleased that you invited us tonight for your holiday. We just wanted to show our appreciation."

Uncle Aaron stood up from the rocking chair and started toward the dining room table. "I don't know about you folks, but I'm starving. What do you say we sit down and get the show on the road?"

They all filed into the crowded dining room and milled around, not sure where to sit. Mrs. Eisenberg took charge, directing four of the Rosenblatts to one side of the table, and seating Dominique next to Sarah on the other side. Mr. Eisenberg sat at the head flanked by Mikey and Mr. Rosenblatt. Uncle Aaron sat opposite him, flanked by Mrs. Rosenblatt and Mrs. Eisenberg. But Mrs. Eisenberg did not stay seated for more than a moment. Once everyone was seated, she got up from her seat and walked over to the brass candlesticks set up on the sideboard next to the window. She placed a white knit kippah on her head and struck a match.

"We'll begin by lighting candles," she announced, not turning around. "Let's hope this will be a New Year filled with light and gladness."

"And good health," piped in Uncle Aaron.

"And good health," echoed Mrs. Eisenberg.

She lit the two small white candles, then blew out the match. Three times she circled her hands in front of the burning candles, then drew her hands over her eyes and began to sing:

"Barukh atah adonay, eloheynu melekh ha-olam, asher kideshanu bemitzvotav, vetzivanu lehadlik ner shel yom tov."

"Blessed are you, Adonay our God," she translated, "Ruler of the universe, who sanctifies us with your commandments, commanding us to light the holiday lights."

Sarah and her dad whispered "Amen," followed by Mikey's high-pitched "Amen" seconds later. Mrs. Eisenberg then recited the Shehekhiyanu prayer, thanking God for bringing them safely to this season, and then returned to her seat.

All during the next part of the meal, as Mr. Eisenberg led their guests through the many rituals—the blessings over the wine, over the washing of hands, over the shiny round hallah, over the apples and honey—Sarah watched her friend out of the corner of her eye. It was hard to tell whether Dominique found this interesting, or just weird. Sarah was dying to ask, but she was afraid of what she'd find out. Besides, there was no way to ask Dominique in front of all these people. How could she give an honest opinion in front of her host and hostess? She was too well brought up to say anything negative even if she was having a horrible time.

But Mikey didn't play by the same rules. As soon as all the blessings were over, he turned to the Rosenblatts and said, "This is fun! Do you like it?"

Dr. Rosenblatt looked quickly at his wife and then at his children. His face said it all: Don't say a word; I'll handle this.

"Yes, Mikey, it's very . . . charming. It's nice to know that some of these old-fashioned customs are still practiced in this day and age."

"Did your family practice any of these . . . customs when you were growing up?" asked Mrs. Eisenberg. Her husband shot her a warning glance, but only Sarah noticed. Mrs. Eisenberg was looking directly at the Rosenblatts.

"My grandparents were Orthodox, so I used to see this kind of thing at their apartment when I visited them," responded Dr. Rosenblatt, "and Janice's mother kept them up until her father died. He was rather rigid about religion. But we ourselves don't go in for that sort of thing. We feel *culturally* Jewish, but we've moved beyond the mumbo-jumbo."

"Mumbo-jumbo, eh?" Uncle Aaron chimed in. "You know what Hitler would have said to that, my friend? Mumbo-jumbo or no mumbo-jumbo, you're still a Jew, and you would have been shoved into the gas-chambers together with your Orthodox cousins. Whether you deny your Judaism or embrace it, it's all the same to the rest of the world."

"How about matzah ball soup?" broke in Mr. Eisenberg nervously. "My wife's matzah balls are legendary."

"Matzah balls!" shouted Mikey, jumping up from his chair. "I want matzah balls!"

Sarah sprang up and tugged at Dominique's sleeve. "Let's go help," she whispered to her friend. "I hate when they get on this topic. Everyone gets so tense and cranky."

The two girls took turns ladling the soup into bowls and carrying it into the dining room. By the time they sat down again, the conversation had turned to more neutral subjects—the stock market, the new suburban shopping mall and its business prospects, Springfield's soccer team. As soon as they saw their chance, Sarah and Dominique excused themselves from the table and went up to Sarah's bedroom.

"God, was that boring!" said Sarah, as she closed and bolted the door behind her. "Grown-ups can talk forever about the dumbest things."

"I know. My parents spend hours discussing furniture and plants. Even Nicole has more interesting things to say."

Sarah walked over to her bed and flopped down on her stomach. "Want to listen to some music? My parents can't hear anything through that door."

"Sure," said Dominique. She sat down on the desk chair, and began playing with the Kooshball on the desk. "Something a bit upbeat after that deadly dinner."

Sarah slipped a CD onto her discman, and heavy metal music began thumping in their ears. "That's better."

They laughed.

"Hey, Sarah, I've been meaning to tell you. Chris's cousin Rick is coming in from Los Angeles in a couple of weeks. I thought it would be fun to double-date."

Sarah said nothing.

Dominique continued. "I've never met Rick, but Chris has told me all about him. He's six feet two, seventeen, with blond hair and loads of muscles. He surfs and drives a motorcycle. Sounds great, huh?"

Still no answer from Sarah.

"Chris says he's got all these connections to Hollywood, too. He's going to try to break into the movies right after high school. Wouldn't that be cool? A movie star!"

While Dominique talked on, Sarah's brain began to race wildly. Never in a million years would her parents let her go out with someone like Rick. A surfer and a biker. Seventeen years old. And certainly not Jewish! Her parents had laid down the law about that. Forget it.

But did they have to know? What harm could it do to go out just once? He didn't even live around here. She'd go out just to have a good time and then he'd go back to Hollywood and she'd never see him again. Except maybe in the movies.

"Yeah, he sounds cool, Dominique. When do you want to go?"

The night of the planned double-date, Sarah was too excited to eat dinner. She had been looking forward to this night for two weeks, ever since Dominique had first told her about Rick. It was hard to believe it was tonight!

She and Dominique had rehearsed every detail of the plan. They would tell their parents they were going to a movie at the Ritz and then were going to meet a few friends for pizza at Al's. Dominique would then come back with Sarah and sleep over so that neither of them would have to travel by public transit alone. They had talked their parents into a midnight curfew.

Except for a few minor details, this *was* the real plan. The minor details were named Chris and Rick.

"What if someone sees me there with Rick?" Sarah had asked Dominique just that morning. "The Ritz is such a public place! It's jammed on Saturday night."

"Just tell them you ran into Rick when you got to the movies. He's someone you once knew from your old school. Or make something else up. Don't obsess over it so much!"

Sarah didn't like to lie. She wasn't very good at it. For one thing, she had such an active imagination that she usually made her lies too complicated, and then couldn't keep track of all the details. For another, her face usually gave her away. She was lousy at pulling a poker face. Even when she was telling the truth she tended to look guilty. She smiled too easily.

But she had no choice this time. If she was ever going to *experience* life fully, she was going to have to break free of her parents' watchful eye. She had to take a few calculated risks, test some limits, test herself. How else would she learn what stuff she was made of?

Feeling her parents' watchful eyes on her right now at the kitchen table, she forced herself to eat a few bites of her father's tuna casserole and several string beans. Then she excused herself and ran to the bathroom to brush her hair for the millionth time that evening. She glanced at her watch. 7:13. Her train downtown was at 7:26. She had better start walking to the station. She was grateful that her parents had consented to let her end Shabbat an hour early.

"Bye, Mom! Bye, Dad! I'll be home at midnight. Don't wait up!"

"Be careful, Sarah!" yelled her mother. "You're not a city girl yet!"

"Have a good time!" her father yelled. "Don't do anything I wouldn't do!"

Sarah slammed the door and hurried down the front steps. It was only a seven-minute walk to the train station but she wasn't taking any chances tonight. She would rather be early than screw things up.

As she rode the high-speed train toward center city, she began fantasizing about her date. Despite his Hollywood good looks, Rick would be more than just a gorgeous body. He would also be smart and funny and sensitive. He would be a great listener and would make Sarah feel perfect instead of like the klutz she was. And he would be romantic but not too fast, even though he was seventeen. He would let Sarah call the shots.

By the time Sarah got to the Ritz box office at eight, the line was halfway around the block. She glanced up and down the line, looking for Dominique, but didn't see her. Now what? What if the show was sold out? What if she had misunderstood the plan and had come to the wrong theater? She began to feel the familiar adrenalin rush of panic in her chest, the racing heartbeat, the difficulty breathing.

"Sarah, over here! We've already bought the tickets!"

The voices were coming from just inside the theater. Dominique was holding open one of the glass doors, a large paper cup of soda in one hand, a large popcorn in the other. She pushed the door open wider with her rear end and beckoned Sarah with a toss of her head. Sarah ran up to her and squeezed by, spilling a few kernels of popcorn as she brushed by her friend.

The lobby was a crush of bodies. Five lines snaked toward the concession stands. Two lines surged forward toward the ticket-takers. Several people leaned over video arcade machines, jabbing buttons and jerking their bodies as they played. Sarah waited for Dominique to join her, then followed her toward two young men standing off to one side, staring at the wall posters. Sarah recognized the shorter one as Chris, Dominique's boyfriend at Springfield. The other one must be Rick.

"Hey, Rick, meet Sarah," announced Dominique.

Rick spun around and faced Sarah. He was even more gorgeous than Sarah had imagined. He had soft gray eyes and seashell white teeth set off by bronze skin. His blond hair was practically white, probably bleached by the California sun. He smiled broadly and stretched out his hand.

"Hello, Sarah. Glad to meet you. Chris has been telling me all about you."

Sarah felt goosebumps prickling her flesh. I can't believe this is happening to me! she thought. It's like being in a movie!

"Hey, let's get on line and get in so we can get seats together," said Chris, moving toward the ticket line. "It looks like a sell-out tonight."

By the time they got into the theater, most of the seats were taken. They couldn't find four together, so they agreed to split up into pairs. Sarah found herself alone with Rick—and she suddenly felt afraid. She hadn't told Dominique the truth—that she had never gone on a real date before, only out with a group. And here she was with an experienced hunk from California. Help!

"Tell me about yourself, Sarah," said Rick as they sat waiting for the previews to begin. "All I know about you is that you're new to the city and that you're pretty."

Sarah blushed. She didn't consider herself pretty. This was probably just a line to win her over. But she didn't care. It felt wonderful!

"I don't know. I like art and writing and animals. And I like to read true-crime novels. I might be a criminologist when I finish college."

Rick laughed. "That's rather unusual. Where I come from everybody wants to either make movies or star in them. I've never met anybody who wanted to be a criminologist."

"Of course, a lot can change between now and later," Sarah added, feeling a little foolish about sharing this fantasy with a total stranger. "It's just an idea I'm trying out."

Then the lights went off, and they sat through the trailers and the movie—a fast-paced adventure with lots of blood and death-defying action—in silence. Sarah was surprised—and maybe even a little disappointed—that during the whole time Rick didn't touch her at all. When the lights came back on, they made their way out into the lobby and waited for Dominique and Chris.

Al's Pizza was a favorite downtown hang-out of high school students. It was close to several movie theaters and stayed open till 2:00 a.m. After a brief wait, they were led to a table in the back, far enough away from the jukebox to hear each other without needing to shout too much.

"What'll ya have?" asked the waitress, a skinny bleached blond with terrible teeth.

"How about a large pepperoni-and-sausage pizza and a pitcher of beer?" Chris asked the girls.

"Got any ID?" muttered the waitress. "Can't serve ya beer without you have some ID."

Chris winked at her. "Don't you believe me, babe?"

"It's the law, mister. Can't serve you beer without you have some ID."

Chris grunted. "OK, make that a pitcher of root beer."

Sarah said softly, "Can we make that just plain pizza?"

"Plain? Al's is famous for their pepperoni-and-sausage pizza. Best in the city!"

"I know, Chris, but I don't eat that stuff."

"Listen, you guys," muttered the waitress, clearly annoyed. "I ain't got all night to wait for youse to make up your mind. I'll come back when youse is ready." And she sauntered off to another table.

"Are these more of your Jewish rules, Sarah?" asked Dominique. "More of what my father calls mumbo-jumbo?"

"It's not mumbo-jumbo, Dominique!" Sarah protested. "Keeping kosher is what Jews do. At least some Jews do," she added when she saw Dominique's frown. "It's part of who I am as a Jew."

"You tell her, Sarah," laughed Rick. "I gotta respect those kinds of principles. You stick up for what you believe. Don't let Dominique here talk you out of it."

"Come on, Rick," said Dominique, "these aren't Sarah's principles. They're her parents'. Sarah's just being a good daughter." She turned toward Sarah. "Time to think for yourself, Sarah. Your parents aren't here tonight. You're on your own."

Sarah shook her head. She was surprised that she was feeling so strongly about keeping kosher. Dominique was right. She was on her own tonight. Her parents didn't even know she was here, dating a non-Jewish boy. But Dominique was wrong about her being just a good daughter. Many of her parents' principles *were* hers now. Just because she didn't agree with her parents about everything didn't mean she couldn't agree with them about some things.

"Sorry, Dominique, I won't eat that stuff. In fact, I don't think I should be here at all. It was a mistake to sneak out like this without telling my parents. If I'm going to go my own way, I've got to do it face to face with them. Not by lying."

And while the other three stared at her with open mouths, she stood up and walked briskly toward the front door. She kept on walking without slowing down until she got to the station. Luckily, the train came within five minutes and she was standing at her front door by 11:30. She turned her key in the lock and slipped quietly inside. She wasn't surprised to find her mother stretched out on the living room couch, reading.

"Hi, Sarah, have a good time?" She paused. "And where's Dominique? I thought you two had planned to come home together."

"Yeah, well, I met this kid from the neighborhood and we rode back together. Nobody you know," she added hastily. Keep it simple, she reminded herself. Don't turn it into a screenplay! "Dominique took a cab home. It's no big deal for her."

"Want to talk about what happened?" asked her mother, as if reading her thoughts.

"Nothing happened, Mom! We just changed our plans, that's all. Well, I'm tired. See you in the morning."

Mrs. Eisenberg stood up and shut off the lamp. "You know what? I'm tired, too. I'm glad you're home safely, Sarah. It's so hard letting you grow up, letting go. I know you have good judgment and will make wise decisions, but I can't help worrying about you. It's a tough world to grow up in these days. I just want you to know that I'll always be here if you want to talk. I was young once, too, you know."

"I know, in prehistoric times." Sarah smiled. "Thanks, Mom. I've got to figure some stuff out by myself. But it's good knowing you're standing by. Just in case."

"Good night, sweets. Sleep late tomorrow. We have nothing planned."

"That's great, Mom. That's my kind of day."

She'd had enough planning to last her for quite some time.

4

The Loss of Free Speech

By mid-October, Sarah was able to catch her breath and begin to relax about school. She had gotten a B+ on her first English paper and had passed her first algebra quiz—just barely, but at least she wasn't going to flunk out. She was deep into her American history project—a study on how the railroad had changed the face of the American West—and had discovered that she was actually enjoying the research, although she dreaded organizing all the notecards together into a term paper.

The one trouble spot was Spanish. At her old school, foreign languages began in eighth grade, but everyone at Springfield had begun in seventh. Her choice had been to go through her new school one year behind her classmates or to try to catch up during her freshman year. At her parents' urging she had decided to try playing catch-up. Given how much homework she was getting, it had probably been a dumb idea.

But if she hadn't agreed to be tutored every day after school, she might not have become friends with Latesha Winters. Latesha was like no one she had ever met before. She was Sarah's first African-American friend. Although there had been a few black students at Franklin Middle School, they had pretty much kept to themselves. Sarah had never even been inside a black person's house. In fact, she had been a little bit scared of black people. They seemed so *different*.

Latesha had changed all that. Every day after last period, they sat together in the cafeteria, drinking Cokes as they plowed through the second-year Spanish book. To their surprise, the two discovered they had a lot in common. For one thing, they both loved animals. Latesha had a dog, a snake, and tropical fish. Sarah had eight mice, two cats, two rabbits, two guinea pigs, and a ferret. Twice, after their lesson, they had gone together to the pet store a few blocks from school to buy food and supplies for their menageries. They even fantasized about opening a pet store together someday. Latesha would run the store while Sarah performed her duties as a zookeeper, then Sarah would take over while Latesha designed buildings in her architecture office. It was a silly idea, of course, but they enjoyed sharing their secret fantasies nonetheless.

But what drew them together even more than their love of animals was their siblings. Like Sarah, Latesha had a younger sibling, Shawna, who was mentally retarded. She sounded so similar to Mikey—seven years old but still only a toddler emotionally and intellectually. Always getting into trouble, breaking things, wandering off at shopping malls, oblivious of danger, too trusting with strangers, adorable and smiley. Mrs. Winters, a divorced single parent, had her hands full taking care of Shawna and working full-time, but Latesha tried to help out whenever she could. Sarah felt a bit guilty that Latesha seemed not to mind helping with her sister as much as she did helping with Mikey.

Either because Latesha was such a good teacher or because Sarah wanted to impress her, Sarah discovered that she was already making great strides in catching up with the freshman Spanish class. Every night just before she went to bed, she listened to tapes in Spanish, hoping that the words might sink into her dreams. She and Latesha practiced the dialogues in homeroom and again right before Spanish class. Just yesterday Señora Fernandez had complimented Sarah on her accent.

Sarah had noticed that Dominique was becoming a little jealous about the rapidly developing friendship between her and Latesha. Dominique was taking French—of course!—not Spanish, and so was shut out of this part of Sarah's life. Not wanting to lose Dominique's friendship, Sarah had gone out of her way to include her as much as possible, although threesomes were rather tricky. At lunch each day, the three sat together. They had gone to the movies together last Saturday night. Tonight they had arranged to have a study marathon at Sarah's house to study for the big history test the next day.

"How much of the test do you think will be multiple-choice?" asked Dominique. She was sprawled on her stomach on Sarah's bed, her elbows propping her up over her open textbook.

"Don't expect more than twenty percent, max," answered Latesha. She was sitting on the floor next to Dominique, leaning against the bed. On her lap was a pile of index cards filled with names and dates. "Steinfeld doesn't believe in regurgitating facts on a test. He's much more interested in essays and analysis. So we should spend most of our time going over the sample questions."

"I hate essay questions!" said Sarah. "You always get penalized more for what you leave out than for what you put in."

"Maybe you just don't know how to study for them," said Latesha. "Let me teach you a few tricks."

"Is that how you do it, Latesha?" asked Dominique, sitting up and arching her back. She let out a loud sigh and flopped over onto her back, hugging one knee, then another to her chest as she talked. "Is that how you ace all those tests—with a few tricks?"

Latesha laughed. "No, Dominique, it's not just a few tricks. I study very hard to get those grades. My mom has threatened to kill me unless I get into a good college and make up for what she didn't get to do with her life. I used to resent that a lot, but now I see that she's really rooting for me to succeed. She doesn't want me to end up in the kind of dead-end job she has."

As always, Sarah admired Latesha's honesty. It must be the way her family operated. No sidestepping the truth. Tell it like it is, and then do something about it. Sarah's own family often talked endlessly *around* a subject without getting to the heart of it. That was probably why Sarah was so afraid of controversy. It seemed so *dangerous*. Why else did her parents avoid conflict like the plague?

"OK, so what are your tricks?" Sarah asked her friend.

Latesha laid the index cards on the carpeted floor and reached for an unopened pack. "Read me the first question."

Sarah stood up and walked over to her desk. Lifting up the photocopied sheet, she read: "What were two of the major causes leading to the Civil War? Choose from among the following categories: economic, political, and social causes. Be specific."

Dominique let out a loud grunt. "Great! A nice little question that only covers about 150 pages in the book. Be specific, he says. Why doesn't he just ask us to memorize the whole book!"

"Take it easy, Dominique," said Latesha, chuckling. "The first trick is learning not to panic. Once you panic, it's all over."

"And the second trick?" asked Sarah, sinking down into her desk chair and throwing one arm over the back. She twisted her head around to look at the two others. "How do you answer a question like that? He'll probably only give us fifteen minutes."

"The secret is asking yourself questions," said Latesha. "Let's say I pick economic and political causes of the Civil War. I ask myself: What did the South gain from slavery? What did it stand to lose if it didn't have it anymore? And how about the North? What did it lose if slavery continued? And what did it stand to gain if it ended?"

"That's a trick? That seems harder than Steinfeld's questions!" exploded Dominique. "I thought you had some shortcuts to help us out."

"I didn't say my tricks made things easier," answered Latesha. "They just help you do well. You still have to study and know the material."

"So what's the answer?" asked Sarah. "What did the South gain by having slaves?"

"Oh, come on, Sarah!" teased Latesha. "You can answer that yourself."

Sarah smiled. "Just testing, Latesha. I guess I would say that the South did pretty well having free labor to plant and harvest the crops. And because the children of slaves belonged to their masters as well, they did better and better the longer slavery lasted. Even if some slaves died because of the horrible conditions, more were born to replace them. It was a better deal than the North had, having to pay workers for their labor."

"Give the girl an A," laughed Latesha. "At this rate, you're going to ruin the curve for the rest of the class. Dr. Steinfeld will be in shock!"

"How late do you kids plan to study?" shouted a woman's voice from downstairs. "I don't want you going past ten."

Sarah glanced up at the large clock on her wall. It was already 8:30 and they had not even gone through all the questions. Despite Latesha's encouragement, she was very nervous about the test tomorrow. This was the first real high school exam she'd ever taken. She wasn't sure she could follow Latesha's first rule and not panic.

"We'll let you know when we're done," shouted Sarah through the closed door. "It shouldn't be too late."

"It *won't* be too late," shouted her mother. "I'm driving your friends home at ten o'clock, Sarah, ready or not."

Sarah stood up and readjusted herself in the chair, sitting down backwards on the seat, straddling it with her legs. "You heard her, Latesha. Ready or not. So, how about a few more tricks?"

The test turned out to be easier than Sarah had expected. Following Latesha's coaching, she worked her way methodically through the essay questions, asking herself a series of smaller questions about each of Dr. Steinfeld's big questions until she felt satisfied that she had answered each one thoroughly. She felt confident that she had done well on the multiple-choice and identification questions as well. Even Dominique, who was usually a nervous wreck about such things, seemed in a good mood as they left the classroom together at the end of the hour.

Three days went by before Dr. Steinfeld had the tests graded and ready to be handed back. At the beginning of the period, he announced that they would go through the essay questions together since so many of the class had not understood what was expected of them. When he said that, Sarah felt the floor drop out of her stomach.

But when she received her paper, she was thrilled to see a big red A- at the top. She had missed several multiple-choice answers and one identification—but had lost no points on the essays. She struggled hard to suppress a wide grin that was threatening to break out on her face. It was clear from looking around the room that most of the others had not been so lucky.

"OK, class, let's look at the first question: 'What were two of the major causes of the Civil War?' Most of you did not supply specific information to back up your generalizations. Some of you missed the point altogether and made up answers that were simply not historically accurate."

"Like me?" sneered a tall, lanky boy from the back of the room.

Everyone whipped around to see who had spoken. It was Jed Hoeflich, a new student at Springfield who had already made many enemies with his rude manners and militaristic clothes.

"Why don't you read out loud what you wrote for your answer, Mr. Hoeflich, and let the class decide about its historical accuracy," said Dr. Steinfeld almost in a whisper. Sarah recognized that quiet tone. Her father used it when he was fighting hard to keep from exploding.

"OK, I will."

He lifted up his paper and drew it close to his face. Sarah figured that he probably needed glasses but was too vain. She had noticed that he was always combing his hair and clipping his nails. He read in a high, whining voice: "The major cause of the Civil War was that the slaves got too big for their britches. They fooled the North into fighting a war for them and then double-crossed them by not making good on their promise to work harder as free men. They should'a stayed slaves. They've ruined America."

No one spoke for several moments after Jed finished reading. Dr. Steinfeld sat silently at his desk, staring blankly at the class. Sarah saw that the knuckles of his right hand were white where they gripped his pen. She glanced over at Latesha. Her friend sat stonily in her chair, holding her breath. Her nostrils flared, and her jaw muscles flexed under her dark skin. But she said nothing. Like Dr. Steinfeld she just stared blankly ahead. Sarah wished her friend would look her way so she could make contact, show her how mad she was, too.

"So, is that what you mean by historically inaccurate, Dr. Steinfeld?" asked Jed, his voice unmistakably sarcastic. "I dare you to prove that I'm wrong!"

"Oh, you're so full of it, Hoeflich!"

Sarah was shocked to hear the words escape from her mouth. Normally she wasn't a very brave person. She almost never spoke first in class, usually waited to be called on. But she was so mad that she couldn't keep the words back. Jed Hoeflich had to be challenged, put in his place.

"Oh, yeah, Eisenberg? Then prove I'm wrong. I dare you!"

Sarah suddenly felt tongue-tied. She couldn't use any of Latesha's tricks now. She was too upset. She could only look over at her friend and imagine her pain. She thought back to the anti-semitic incidents earlier that year involving Dominique, to her own run-in with Crystal and her friends. And that had not been as *public* as what was happening now. How dare Jed Hoeflich say what he'd said!

"Listen, Jed, I know all about prejudice and slavery. The Jews have been the target of lies like yours for centuries. It's very convenient to blame the victims instead of looking at what makes them behave the way they do. Black people were brought to this country in chains, against their will, separated from their families, their languages, their religions; then worked like animals till they died or gave up hoping for freedom. Whatever is ruining America is all of our faults, and all of our responsibilities to fix."

"Nice speech, Eisenberg!" said Jed, smirking. "My dad's right. Jews and blacks are both out to steal America blind. Parasites, that's what you are, parasites."

At that the class erupted. Dr. Steinfeld shouted for order but no one listened. One girl sitting right behind Sarah yelled: "This guy should be suspended as a racist and antisemite! He doesn't belong here!"

"Yeah, kick 'im out!"

"He should be shot!"

During the commotion, Jed Hoeflich sat back in his chair, surprisingly calm, even smiling as the class became more agitated. He took out his nail clipper and began paring his nails, glancing up every once in a while to look at Dr. Steinfeld, who sat rigidly at his desk, silent again after his call for order had failed.

Finally, the cries died down and everyone looked toward the teacher at the front of the room. He stood up slowly and said, "One of the great treasures of this great country of ours is its

Constitution, which we studied at considerable length just a few weeks ago. One of the freedoms guaranteed by that remarkable document is freedom of speech. Mr. Hoeflich has just proven just how extraordinary this right is. It protects an individual's right to voice even the most offensive opinions—as long as such opinions do not endanger the public welfare."

Again Sarah felt herself compelled to speak.

"Dr. Steinfeld, I can't believe that the people who wrote the Constitution had someone like Jed Hoeflich in mind when they discussed freedom of speech. Lies and hate speech don't belong in any country, even a democracy."

"I'm afraid that I have to disagree with you, Sarah. As much as I share your disgust at Mr. Hoeflich's remarks—and as a Jew, I feel them as personally as you do—I must defend his right to express them. However, as his teacher I reserve the right to fail him on the grounds of historical inaccuracy. He can think and say whatever he likes, but he cannot get away with passing lies off as facts."

"You still haven't proven me wrong, Dr. Steinfeld," sneered Jed. "I think I deserve full credit for my answer."

"We can talk about this after class, Jed. I'd like to move on to some other students' answers."

"Oh, no, you don't!" shouted Jed. "You're not going to weasel out of this so easily."

"Why don't you just shut up!" screamed Sarah, standing at her place and shaking a fist toward the back of the room. "You love all this attention, don't you? Well, maybe you should get your own TV show and froth at the mouth there!"

"Sarah, Jed, I said that's enough now," said Dr. Steinfeld, his voice rising. "I said I wanted to move on . . ."

"You may want to move on, Dr. Steinfeld, but I'm not going to let him get away with this!" Sarah was almost crying now, she was so angry.

Jed laughed loudly and pointed at Sarah. "You're turning red, Eisenberg! You'd better watch out or you'll explode!"

Dr. Steinfeld slammed both hands down on the wooden desk. "OK, that's it! Both of you have detention today. You will report to Mr. Johnson's office at 2:45." He stopped and took a deep breath, sitting back down in his chair. "Now—can we please get on with the class?"

Sarah also sat down, breathing hard. She could feel the warmth in her cheeks. She saw Latesha staring at her, her eyes glistening as though on the verge of tears. Despite the detention, despite Dr. Steinfeld's stern reprimand, Sarah felt good about what she had just done. It was the first time she had ever done anything like that. And no matter what anyone else said, she knew she had done the right thing. And that felt great.

Latesha was waiting outside the school building at four o'clock when Sarah finished detention. As Sarah walked toward her, she held out a can of diet Coke in one hand and a doughnut in the other. Sarah smiled, took her friend's offering with a nod, and they began walking together toward the train station.

"Well . . . ?" Latesha finally broke the silence.

"Well, what?"

"Aren't you going to yell at me for not standing up to that creep in class?"

Sarah's smile widened. She took a long sip of her soda, spilling a little down the front of her T-shirt as her foot hit an uneven spot in the pavement. She blotted the wet spot with the edge of her shirt.

"Why would I do a thing like that?" she exclaimed. "Honestly, Latesha, your mind works in the strangest way!"

Latesha grinned sheepishly. "Well, you should hear what my other friends said to me at lunch when word about what happened got around. You'd think I'd just sold out my entire people!"

"Hey, how can I get on your case? Normally, I'm the biggest coward of them all. I don't really understand what got into me today, why Hoeflich made me so mad that I couldn't keep my mouth shut."

"Well, I'm sure glad that you couldn't, 'cause I would've felt pretty rotten if no one had stood up to him. I don't think I ever heard such poisonous garbage in my life!"

"I was kind of surprised at Steinfeld," said Sarah, taking a bite out of her doughnut. "I didn't think he would be so . . . neutral. I mean, he's Jewish!"

They reached the stairs leading down to the regional rail station and descended below street level. This was later than their usual train home. The station was already filling up with commuters, rushing headlong past the two teenagers, the men in dark suits and grasping briefcases, the women in lighter suits or fashionable dresses, toting bulging leather briefcases in one hand, hanging on to their shoulderbags with the other. Sarah and Latesha hugged the corridor wall to avoid the crush.

"What'd you do in detention?" asked Latesha as they sat down side by side on a square wooden cube in the middle of the platform to await their train.

"Nothing, really. We just sat in the lobby near the front desk and did our homework. Mr. Johnson was too busy to give us one of his famous lectures. Jed kept looking over at me. I don't know what he expected to see, but he stopped when I stuck out my tongue at him."

They both laughed.

"I know that was immature, but it seemed so . . . appropriate."

"And that's all that happened?"

Sarah took one last swig from her can and then tossed it into the trash can nearby. They now heard the distant rumble of their train, then saw the white headlight approaching. They were swept along onto the rear car and pushed forward. It was a few moments before they found seats near each other and resumed their conversation.

"Johnson came out at about a quarter to four and told us that he had called our parents and asked them to come in first thing tomorrow morning. My dad will not be pleased, I can tell you that. He hates being late for work."

"What's he going to talk to them about? Are you going to be suspended?"

Sarah shrugged. "I doubt it. I bet we'll just hear a lecture about tolerance and respect for members of the school community. You've heard it all before, believe me."

Then it was Latesha's stop, and they said goodbye. Sarah didn't mind riding the rest of the way home crowded among strangers. Sometimes it was nice being anonymous.

At 8:45 the next morning, Sarah and her parents stood awkwardly in the doorway to Mr. Johnson's office, a spacious, tastefully decorated corner room on the first floor. The principal's massive desk and two walls of bookcases were made of shiny rich mahogany. In front of the desk stood a semicircle of simple wooden chairs, armless, with gray cloth seats. Sarah counted six of them. For the two culprits and their parents.

"Come in, come in!" Mr. Johnson cried when he looked up from the papers he was reading and noticed them. He came forward, reaching out for their hands and then beckoning them in with a grand sweep of his right arm. He was a big man, beefy and good-humored, with light curly hair and glasses. Most of the students found him somewhat overbearing, but he was generally well liked. He was fair and tough, a good combination for a high school principal.

"Sit wherever you like," he said, pointing directly to the three chairs in the left arc of the semicircle. Sarah sat in the middle of the three. Her parents sat down on either side of her. For several minutes they sat without speaking, waiting. Mr. Johnson went back to his paperwork, apparently oblivious of their presence.

A knock on the door broke the silence.

Mr. Johnson sprang up and rushed to the door to let the Hoeflichs in. They were a sour-looking group—Jed, tall and skinny, with squinty eyes and very short dark hair; his father, similarly tall and skinny, wearing glasses and the same cropped hairstyle; Mrs. Hoeflich, petite, her facial features birdlike, sharp and nervous.

"Come in, come in," cried Mr. Johnson, showing them to the other set of three chairs. Sarah felt like she was on some sort of TV game show. They were two panels of contestants, vying for washing machines and camcorders. Mr. Johnson was the jolly host, whose real job was to sell toothpaste and new cars.

"Well, why are we here today?" began the principal, settling back down in his swivel chair behind the desk. He touched his fingertips to each other so that they formed a vaulted roof over his prominent belly. His gaze settled on Sarah, then swiveled over to Jed, then back again to Sarah. "So, why don't one of you young people begin?"

Sarah and Jed looked at each other—or more accurately, glared at each other, then looked away. Mr. Johnson watched them closely, smiling.

"Oh, come, come, Sarah, Jed, let's be mature about this, shall we?"

Still neither of them volunteered to begin the conversation. It was Mr. Hoeflich who broke the ice.

"From what my son tells me, there seems to be some problem in this school tolerating different opinions."

Mr. Johnson leaned forward, his smile replaced by concern. "Could you be more specific, Mr. Hoeflich?"

"Jed tells me that he was shouted down for giving his version of what happened in the Civil War. Seems everyone's too politically correct"—he pronounced these last two words with an exaggerated southern drawl, clipping the consonants so that the words sounded like machine-gun fire—"to allow a different way of looking at things. Sounds like censorship to me."

"Is that so, Jed?" asked Mr. Johnson, leaning back in his chair and swiveling slowly from side to side.

"Yeah, that's right," said Jed, looking up at his father, who nodded to him, smiling grimly. "People just couldn't stand to hear the truth."

"It wasn't the truth, Jed!" burst out Sarah. Her father touched her gently on the shoulder, then raised his eyebrows when she looked back at him. "I'm sorry, Dad. I won't let him pull this again. I'm not going to listen to his lies about black people being responsible for the mess our country's in now. That's just outright racism, not a different interpretation of history!"

"Excuse me, Sarah," said Mr. Johnson, leaning forward again and smiling gently. "I can understand your feelings, but I want this to be a fair hearing this morning. I want both sides to have a chance to tell their stories."

"I'm sure Sarah wants that, too," said Mrs. Eisenberg, patting her daughter lightly on the hand. "Sarah's a big believer in the free exchange of ideas." She winked at her daughter, who scowled back at her. "In fact, our home is the testing ground for that philosophy."

Mr. Johnson and the Eisenbergs laughed. But the Hoeflichs sat with grim expressions on their faces as if they were all carved out of stone. Sarah looked at her watch and began to count under her breath. How much longer, she thought. How much longer till he lets us go?

"Well, be that as it may," declared Mr. Johnson to no one in particular. "Where do we go from here?"

"I would like to make it very clear," said Mrs. Hoeflich in a chirpy voice, "that Clyde and I are very displeased with Springfield's handling of this matter. I was led to believe when we enrolled Jed here that there was sufficient diversity so that our son would feel at home. I can see that this is not the case."

"Mrs. Hoeflich," said Mr. Johnson. Sarah couldn't tell whether he was annoyed or worried. His eyebrows were squeezed together over his nose like caterpillars kissing. "I can assure you that diversity is valued very highly here at Springfield. But so is tolerance and respect. I understand that your son said some rather harsh words about various ethnic groups."

"You mean Negroes and Jews?" snapped Mr. Hoeflich. As one, Mr. and Mrs. Eisenberg and Mr. Johnson sucked in their breaths in a loud whoosh. Sarah glanced over at the Hoeflichs. They were smiling smugly, all three of them, especially Jed, who was looking up at his father with undisguised admiration.

"That is precisely what I was referring to, Mr. Hoeflich," said Mr. Johnson curtly. "We do not approve of such opinions here."

"So I was right!" cried Mr. Hoeflich. "You do practice censorship here!"

"Not censorship, Mr. Hoeflich. Mutual respect. Each individual is valued for who he or she is."

"I think I've heard enough," declared Mrs. Hoeflich, rising suddenly from her chair. "Back where we come from, we believe in calling a spade a spade."

Jed snorted. "Yeah, back home, we sure do call a spade a spade." He snickered.

Sarah opened her mouth, then shut it with a loud snap. "You're disgusting, Jed, you know that! Disgusting!"

"Huh, I'd like to see you call me that back home. My daddy would call the boys together so fast . . ."

He stopped abruptly when his father reached down and grasped his forearm.

"I think we've said enough, son." He stood up and turned to face Mr. Johnson. "As of today, we are withdrawing Jed from your school, sir. He cannot learn in an environment that discourages free speech. My wife and I will make inquiries about other schools in the area, or if need be, make arrangements for

Jed to board in an appropriate school. My family warned me that it might be like this up here, but frankly, I'm still shocked to discover it myself."

Stiffly, the three Hoeflichs made their way to the door and exited. Jed closed the door behind him with a slam.

"Where did they come from?" asked Mrs. Eisenberg, shuddering.

"Some primeval swamp, I suspect," said Mr. Johnson. No one laughed. "I must confess that we've never had a student like that at Springfield before. They usually know better than to come to us, since we have a reputation for liberal ideas. But I guess someone steered them wrong." He leaned over toward Sarah.

"I couldn't say this before when the Hoeflichs were here, Sarah, but I want to tell you how proud I am of you. It took a lot of guts to stand up to someone like Jed Hoeflich in front of the whole class, especially since you're still new here. You did us all proud—even if you did wind up with detention." He winked.

Sarah smiled. "I really did it for Latesha, Mr. Johnson. She must really have been hurt by what Jed said if she couldn't even talk back for herself. That's not like her. She's really a strong person. But I guess we're all afraid of something."

"Even the Hoeflichs," said Mr. Eisenberg, shaking his head. "They're afraid of what our country has become, a real rainbow of cultures. Where they come from, the differences are less visible than they are in a big city like ours. People like the Hoeflichs are afraid to acknowledge that America doesn't only belong to white people anymore—or to any one privileged group. We all have to figure out how to share it—or we all lose it."

"I thought the Civil War settled all that already," said Sarah.

Mr. Johnson smiled. "I'm glad you recognize that your history lessons *are* relevant, Sarah. I'm afraid that wars don't often settle things once and for all. More often they simply call a truce for a time. Like we just did in this office. Jed will go to another school and continue to believe what he believes. Maybe someday he'll make a friend like Latesha and realize how wrong he's been. Or maybe he won't. All we can do here is to state the truth as we see it. As you did yesterday."

He came out from behind his desk and reached out a beefy hand. "I'm glad you're here, Sarah. Springfield is lucky to have you."

"Thanks, Mr. Johnson. I'm glad I'm here, too. Now can I go to first period? I've got a biology quiz."

The three adults laughed. Mr. Johnson nodded to her and she sprang up out of her chair.

"You tell it like it is, Sarah!" shouted her father as she rushed out the door. "Tell the truth about those paramecia!"

5

A Special Kind of Love

Even though it was late November, the weather was still glorious—brisk but clear and sunny. Most of the leaves were gone from the trees, revealing lumpy bird and squirrel nests in many of the branches. At the train station where Sarah and Mikey waited for the train, a few brittle brown leaves swirled at their feet, making scratchy sounds as they scraped along the concrete pavement. Sarah's nose twitched as she smelled the sharp tang of urine in the open shelter behind her. She noticed the graffiti covering the blank wooden walls, the mustaches on the men and women in the posters advertising haircuts and fancy clothes. The fallout of urban life.

Since it was Sunday, there was no one else on the platform. She kept a sharp eye on Mikey, who was poking a stick in a hole near the edge of the platform. Mikey loved taking the train. He still called it a "choo-choo train," and clapped his hands every time he saw it coming. It was very different from the bus that he rode every day to the special school he attended or the family car. The train was an adventure, a rare treat.

Sarah had not really wanted to take her brother downtown on this Sunday morning, but she'd agreed when her parents had pleaded with her—and bribed her with the promise of dinner at her favorite Italian restaurant later that week. Besides, they argued, it was the Sunday after Thanksgiving, so she had no confirmation class. And they had a wedding to go to, and no one to stay with Mikey. So Sarah had grudgingly agreed to take him to a movie downtown and then for a treat nearby.

The good part about it was that she had convinced Latesha to come along with her sister. The movie wasn't until after church, and Mrs. Winters was delighted at the prospect of a free Sunday afternoon. It would give her a chance to visit her sick mother in the hospital and catch up with her bills.

A slight vibration under her feet and a faint clack-clack-clack alerted Sarah that the train was approaching. She looked around for Mikey, and panicked when she couldn't see him.

"Mikey!" she cried, leaning over the track to see the white headlight growing larger as the train sped toward the station. "Mikey! Where are you?"

Mikey came out from behind the shelter carrying two fistfuls of gleaming horse chestnuts. He held them out to Sarah, who let out a loud puff of relief, and then exploded in anger.

"Mikey! Bad boy! How many times have I told you to stay near me when we go on trips, especially when we're at the train station? You gave me such a scare!"

Mikey hung his head and began to whimper. He opened his fists and let the nuts tumble to the concrete, where they bounced in all directions. She saw his lower lip tremble. Immediately she felt guilty. Mikey hadn't deliberately done anything wrong. He was doing the best he could.

"Never mind, Mikey," she said, stroking his soft brown hair.

The eight-year-old boy looked up at her and smiled broadly. Then he heard the train. The smile turned to ecstasy when he saw the two-car commuter train pulling up to the platform. He began to jump up and down, his movements clumsy and comical, clapping his hands and chanting, "Choo-choo train! Choo-choo train!"

The conductor leapt off the train and shouted, "Center city!"

Mikey ran toward the lower step of the first car. The conductor reached out and helped him up, giving him a slight push from behind as Mikey pulled himself up the three steps by the slim steel handrail. Sarah scrambled on behind him, thanking the conductor with a nod. She entered the almost empty car and found Mikey already seated by a window, his small nose pressed up against the dirty window peering out.

"What do you see, Mikey?" she asked him.

"Train station," he replied, pointing. "See the nuts I dropped."

"Sorry about that, Mikey. I didn't mean to make you drop them."

Mikey didn't seem to hear her. As the train pulled slowly out of the station, he began bouncing up and down on the long seat. His breath clouded the lower half of the window and he craned his neck to see above it.

Sarah dug around in her purse for her wallet. When she found it, she took out her monthly rail pass and slipped it under the metal tongue screwed into the seat top in front of her. She looked at her watch. Fourteen minutes until Latesha's stop. She would be glad to have her company.

The conductor came around to check tickets. He nodded to Sarah when he saw her pass, and smiled when he saw Mikey, still bouncing on the seat beside her.

"Hi, big fella," he said in a too friendly tone. "Whatcha see?"

"The zoo!" cried Mikey. "I see the zoo!"

Sarah felt embarrassed by her brother's loudness. He would have to learn not to be so *public*. Despite all the programs these days about Down's syndrome kids, the Special Olympics, the new laws, kids like Mikey were still misunderstood and laughed at. Her parents were always reminding people that Mikey could see and hear perfectly well, that he had feelings too. They lectured Sarah all the time that she had to be his strongest advocate—especially after they were gone. Sarah hated to hear that, but she knew that they were only thinking of Mikey's welfare.

"Sit down, Mikey, and I'll show you where we're going today."

Curious, Mikey plopped down beside her on the seat. He peered over her arm at the small newspaper clipping on her lap. The picture showed several cartoon characters—a duck, a donkey, an ostrich, a panda—dancing around a tree, holding hands, or more accurately, paws and wings. Mikey smiled and looked up at his big sister.

"Read me," he said. "Read me what it says."

Sarah read: "'International Festival of Animation.' That means cartoons, Mikey. It's a lot of different cartoons from all over the world." She continued when she saw that her brother was not going to respond: "'Today at the Century Theater. 2 p.m. to 4 p.m. Price of admission—$6.75 for adults, $5.00 students and senior citizens, children under 12 free.' That's you, Mikey. You're free."

Mikey began pointing at the cartoon animals in the ad. "Read me about them."

"There's nothing about them in here, Mikey. It's just an ad for the movie. This must be one of the cartoons."

Mikey's face fell in disappointment. He started playing with a thread dangling from the back of the seat in front of him. Sarah gently pulled his hand away before he did any damage.

"Chelten Avenue next!" cried the conductor. "Chel . . . ten!"

Sarah glanced at her watch. Latesha's stop, finally. She looked over Mikey's head to see if she could see her friend on the platform below. No sign of her. Was she going to miss the train? It was probably her sister's fault. Sarah knew how hard it was to get her own brother from one place to the next on time. It took incredible planning—and luck.

No, there she was, running up the walk, dragging Shawna behind her. The little girl was blubbering and pulling back on her sister's hand. Sarah hoped the conductor would see them before the train pulled off. She reached over Mikey's head and banged on the window. The conductor looked up at the train. Sarah pointed at Latesha and Shawna, who were making slow progress toward the platform. He smiled and nodded. Sarah relaxed and sat back.

It took several minutes before Latesha and Shawna came into the car and made their way to where Sarah and Mikey were sitting. Shawna had stopped crying and was sucking contentedly on a lollipop. Latesha held a purple lollipop out to Mikey, who grabbed it excitedly and thrust it into Sarah's face so that she could unwrap it. Soon he too was sucking happily on the candy.

Sarah and her friend looked at each other and laughed.

"I thought I'd never make it in time," panted Latesha, flopping down beside Sarah on the long seat. Shawna sat across the aisle at the window, staring outside. "Everything was fine until we got near the station. Then Shawna decided that she didn't want to go on the train and began to fight me. It took all my strength to get her up that little hill."

"They're something else, aren't they?" said Sarah, giggling. "I don't know how people do this for a living, taking care of lots of these kids or teaching them."

"Oh, they're better than a lot of kids," said Latesha, her breathing at last back to normal. "I mean, you have to admit that Shawna and Mikey are loving and lovable. They may be slow but they're super-sweet. Better that than smart and mean."

"Ticket?" asked the conductor, stopping by Latesha.

Latesha rummaged around in her pocket and pulled out a rail pass protected by clear plastic. She pointed to her sister at the opposite window. "She's with me."

"Thanks," said the conductor, nodding. Then he bellowed: "Next stop—North Philadelphia!

Shawna tore her gaze from the window and stared at the conductor, startled. Latesha slid over from her seat and hugged her. "It's OK, Shawnie. The man is just telling people where the train is going next. He didn't mean to scare you."

Shawna nodded and was soon pressed up against the window again. Latesha returned to her place next to Sarah.

"How do you do that, Latesha?" asked Sarah. "Can you read her mind or something?"

Latesha laughed. "Sure. It's part of my training. I bet you can do the same with Mikey."

"Not really. Since Mikey's only been with us for two years, it's harder to know what makes him tick. Mom's the best at it. Dad and I have to try much harder, and sometimes we just don't have a clue. I hope it'll get easier as he gets older."

Latesha looked over at Shawna, then at Mikey. "For us, probably. But not for them. If anything, things will get harder. At least now they're cute. When they get older, they'll just seem retarded. Then they'll need us more than ever."

Sarah was surprised to hear Latesha say that. She sounded just like her parents. But coming from her friend, it didn't sound like a lecture. It just sounded right. Sarah glanced over at her brother, still sucking on his lollipop. You can count on me, Mikey, she thought to herself. I'll be there for you, even after they're gone.

It was a madhouse at the Century Theater by the time they got there. It seemed as if every kid in the city had converged on the place. There were also quite a few teenagers and adults. That made Sarah feel better.

It was a few minutes before two, and people were still rushing up to the box office. Latesha volunteered to get the tickets while Sarah watched Mikey and Shawna. Sarah wasn't sure which was the harder job.

As soon as she was left alone with Mikey and Shawna near the front doors of the theater, Sarah felt a tug at her arm. It was Mikey, his face screwed up in pain.

"I gotta pee!" he wailed.

"Oh, no, Mikey," moaned Sarah. "You're just going to have to wait a few more minutes till they open the doors."

"I gotta pee now!"

"There's nothing I can do now," Sarah said. "We can't go in yet."

"Me, too!" chimed in Shawna, although her face, in contrast to Mikey's, bore a cheerful smile. "I gotta pee, too!"

Sarah's mind went into overdrive. Now what? She could take them over to the tree at the curbside and let Mikey pee there in front of all these people, but that was asking for trouble. She could knock on the doors and explain to the ushers that she had an emergency. They probably wouldn't buy it. Kids must try that trick all the time to get in before the crowd. She spotted a McDonald's across the street. She could take them there, but they might not get back in time to get decent seats, and Latesha would never be able to save three seats in such a packed crowd.

Mikey pulled on her sleeve again.

"I gotta pee!"

Sarah noticed that the urgency was gone from his voice. She smelled a slight whiff of urine. Too late. Luckily the smell was mild. She hoped no one noticed.

Latesha came up just then with the tickets. She too smelled the faint odor coming from Mikey.

"Oh, Mikey, how could you!"

Mikey smiled at her, apparently pleased with himself and obviously relieved. He turned around and began looking at the brightly colored posters behind the glass display windows on the walls outside the theater. Shawna soon joined him, her need for a bathroom now forgotten.

Sarah whispered to Latesha. "Mikey's been having problems with keeping himself dry lately. We think it's the new teacher at his school. He's never adjusted well to change. He's wearing diapers until he gets himself back under control. I'll change him once we're inside."

Yuchh, thought Sarah. This was how it had been when Mikey had first arrived at their home two years ago. Her little brother had taken months to get used to a new family, new surroundings, a new routine. Luckily, once he had stabilized—that was the social worker's word—he had not needed diapers again. Until now.

"Hey, what's that awful stink?" shouted a male voice nearby.

Sarah looked around and saw a group of teenage boys staring at them from a few feet away. One was pointing at Mikey and holding his nose with his other hand. The others began to imitate him, laughing noisily.

Mikey began to cry when he looked up and saw them laughing and pointing at him. Sarah ran up to her brother and hugged him close to her.

The boy who had first spoken, walked—or rather, swaggered—over to Latesha and Shawna. He was big and scary, with broad shoulders and a small silver skull dangling from one ear. He was dressed completely in black—leather jacket, tight black jeans, black boots. A dragon's head tattoo peeked out from under his jacket collar.

"What happened? Your little brother have a little accident?" he asked, glancing back as he spoke to his friends, who roared with crude laughter.

"I don't see why it's any business of yours," retorted Latesha. She walked over, placing one arm protectively around Mikey's shoulder.

"Well, I'm making it my business, sister, 'cause I'm about to go in and watch some movies and I don't want no stinky kid ruinin' my enjoyment."

Again the roar from his pals. Sarah moved closer to Latesha, although a voice inside told her to run. Mikey appeared oblivious to what was going on. He let Sarah guide him to another poster closer to the front doors.

"I'll . . . I'll take care of the odor when we get inside," Sarah stammered, inching away. "And you don't have to sit anywhere near us if you don't want to."

The big stranger came nearer, leaned over toward Mikey and stared at him. Then, as if a bulb had lit up, he brightened and backed away, holding his nose.

"Now I get it! Your brother's a retard! He probably pees in his pants all the time! Don't you, moron?"

Mikey buried his face in Sarah's jacket, his shoulders shaking as he began to sob. Latesha's face hardened, her eyes narrowing and her mouth tightening as though drawn taut by a string.

"What do you know about it?" she snapped. "From the way you're acting, I'd say you don't rank very high in the intelligence department yourself. You *or* your friends!"

The boy in black threw back his head and hooted, setting off an echo of hoots from his friends. The group moved forward until it joined up with its leader, and then they all began to move slowly forward, like a dark stain spreading through cloth. Latesha walked up to Sarah and pulled her elbow, moving the four of them backward toward the locked glass doors.

Just then, one of the doors opened, and the theater manager stepped out. Not looking where she was going, Sarah bumped into him and let out a high squeal. He was about to scold her when he saw the ugly knot of teenage boys approaching, threatening, closing in fast on the two friends and their younger siblings.

"Please help us," pleaded Sarah. "Those guys are out to get us!"

From the approaching boys came low, snarling voices:

"Let's get the retards!"

"Yeah, they're subhumans. They can't even feel pain."

"Let's put 'em out of their misery!"

The manager stepped out from behind Sarah and held out his hand. The boys stopped in their tracks. But their faces did not lose their ugly menace.

"What seems to be the problem, boys?" he asked in a neutral tone.

"Nothin', mister. We just don't want no stinkin' retard ruinin' the show for us."

It was the leader who spoke. His friends nodded their heads vigorously in agreement.

The manager turned back toward Sarah. "I do detect a certain . . . aroma coming from your brother, young lady."

Sarah smiled weakly. "I'll take care of that as soon as we're inside. I promise the smell will be gone before we sit down."

The manager smiled back. He bent toward her and whispered, "My nephew is a special-needs child. I know what it's like. I give you a lot of credit."

He walked a few steps toward the group of boys and stopped, placing his hands on his hips.

"You heard the young woman. She'll take care of the problem inside. So I don't want any trouble from *you*."

"From us?" jeered the boy in black. "You've got some nerve, mister! You let a retard stink up your theater and you tell us you don't want no trouble from us? You got it all wrong, you know that, all wrong!"

"Since it is my theater, gentlemen," the manager said coolly, "I am going to exercise my prerogative as the proprietor to bar you from entering during this show. By your rude behavior, you have just forfeited your tickets."

"Hey, you can't do that!"

The manager smiled. "Oh, yes, I can. The theater code specifies that I can take necessary precautions to protect the public safety. And I see you as a threat to that safety."

The ringleader twirled around on one heel and shouted to his friends. "Come on, you guys, we don't have to waste no more time on this wimpy show. We got better things to do." He called back over his shoulder, "You'll be sorry, mister. Real sorry! I hope you got good insurance!"

Laughing, the group headed toward the street. The manager walked over to the glass doors, went in through the one he had come out of, and then proceeded to unlock the rest one by one. The crowd surged forward and poured into the theater, Sarah, Latesha, Mikey, and Shawna in the lead. Latesha and Shawna headed toward the huge auditorium to find four seats, while Sarah and Mikey made a beeline for the ladies' room. The first cartoon had just begun when Sarah and her brother sat down next to Latesha and her sister in one of the front rows. Sarah breathed in deeply through her nose. She smelled soap and baby powder. And an ocean of buttered popcorn.

Sarah was surprised by how good the animation festival was. Unlike the silly cartoons that Mikey watched every weekday afternoon and on Sunday mornings, these were quite clever. Some were political satires, some were familiar stories, some were even jokes. She loved the claymation ones where clay figures seemed to have a life of their own.

Mikey and Shawna didn't really care what the movies were about. They just loved to watch the lively movement and the bright colors. Sarah and Latesha had to keep "shushing" them because they cried out each time they saw something they recognized—an animal, a choo-choo train, a flower. Fortunately, lots of other kids were making noise, so Mikey and Shawna weren't singled out as they sometimes were in an audience.

"Well, how about some ice cream?" offered Sarah as they exited the dark theater into the lowering autumn sun. "We can go to the Big Scoop. It's right around the corner."

Shawna and Mikey both began to clap their hands and jump up and down. They headed down the block toward the ice cream shop, holding each other's hands. The crowd had rapidly dissipated after the movie let out, and the city streets were almost deserted.

When they saw the oversized ice cream cone sign hanging up half a block away, the two younger children began to run toward it. They burst into the shop, startling the few customers at tables and at the counter. By the time Sarah and Latesha entered a few moments later, they were sitting opposite each other at a back table, pointing excitedly at the brightly colored pictures on the menu. A waiter hurried over to them, looking relieved as their older siblings joined them at the table.

"Uh, do you need some time before you order?" he asked. He was a high school kid, about Sarah and Latesha's age although his short height and high voice made him seem younger.

"Sure, give us about five minutes," answered Latesha.

"I want that!" yelled Mikey, pointing to an extravagant gooey concoction on the back page of the plastic-coated menu. Sarah gasped when she saw that Mikey's choice, "The Dieter's Nightmare," cost $8.95.

"How about something a bit . . . smaller, Mikey? It's too close to dinner for so much ice cream." She flipped his menu and pointed to "The Conehead," a scoop of ice cream in a dish, with an inverted cone for a hat, and a face made of Reese's Pieces and whipped cream. Every time they went to a restaurant they went through a similar routine: Mikey would select the most expensive, most elaborate dessert on the menu, and Sarah or her parents would have to talk him into a more reasonable choice.

Luckily, he was easily convinced. As was Shawna. When the waiter returned, Sarah quickly ordered two coneheads for Mikey and Shawna and two dishes of ice cream for herself and Latesha. They settled into their treats without talking, the younger children noisily chomping on their ice cream and toppings, Latesha and Sarah quietly spooning up theirs. By this time, the restaurant was deserted except for their table. It was the dead of a fall Sunday afternoon.

When the bell above the front door jangled, it was Mikey who looked up first and noticed who it was.

"Bad men!" he yelled, pointing. "Go away, bad men!"

The other three looked up. It was the boy in black with his thugs. They grinned when they saw Mikey and the others, and began moving toward the back of the small restaurant.

"Wellll . . ." drawled the ringleader, coming right up to their table and pulling up a chair. He twirled the chair so that its back leaned against the table, then straddled the seat, leaning his forearms on the rounded chrome arc of the chair back. "If it isn't the retards and their bodyguards."

The others crowded closer, sitting down at nearby tables. The waiter nervously approached one of the tables, his pad poised to take their orders. They waved him away. He scurried behind the counter and busied himself refilling the ice cream bins behind the glass display.

"What do you want?" asked Latesha. Her voice was calm, but the hand holding the spoon shook slightly.

"What makes you think I want anything?" The boy's voice was smooth but threatening. It had a growl in it, like a fan on low speed.

"What do you want?" repeated Latesha. Shawna huddled close to her, grasping her upper arm and whimpering. Mikey looked up at Sarah, unsure about what was happening.

"Well, if you're in a giving mood, friends, we sure would like to get our money back from that thee-ater. We were countin' on seeing those movies, and then that mean man threw us out. For no good reason."

Sarah quickly did the calculation in her head. There were five of them, five times $6.75—that added up to $33.75! She didn't have that kind of money on her. And it was unlikely that Latesha did, either.

"I don't have it," Sarah blurted out. "I only have enough to pay for my brother's and my share of the ice cream. I don't have much more than that."

"Me neither," said Latesha, her voice barely audible.

"Oh, that's really too bad," the boy said, with mock concern. "Me and my buddies could use the money to get us some ice cream and sodas. We would hate to be disappointed."

"I told you we don't have it!" insisted Sarah, her voice rising into a whine. "What do you want us to do about it?"

"Glad you asked," said the boy, standing up and beckoning to his friends to come closer. "Tell you what. I can see that you're honest kids, so we'll trust you to go home and get the money and bring it back."

"Go home!" cried Latesha. "It would take over an hour to do that—and with the Sunday trains running so infrequently, it might be much longer."

"An hour, eh?"

"Come on, Ice!" protested one of the boys at another table. "I don't got time to wait around for no hour!"

"OK, OK, let's try a different idea. Tell you what," again the tone of mock concern, with a nasty edge to it, "whatcha got of value on you—watches, necklaces, earrings, credit cards?"

They gave him what they had, emptying their pockets onto the table. Mikey began to cry when Sarah's wallet knocked over his ice cream, spilling it. A chocolate river snaked toward the edge of the table and cascaded over onto the floor.

"Shut up, retard!" yelled the boy as he rummaged hastily through the mess on the table, "or I'll give you something to really cry about."

His words only made Mikey cry louder. Now Shawna added her loud voice to her friend's, and the two of them soon drowned out the soft rock music in the background. Sarah glanced over at the counter. The cashier and the waiter both were riveted to where they stood, watching the scene, frozen in fear.

"What're you guys staring at?" shouted one of the boys. "Bring us some menus so's we can order!"

"I've got to go to the ladies' room," said Sarah in a small voice. Mikey grabbed onto her, shaking his head. "You can come with me, Mikey," she said gently. He relaxed his grip, but did not let go.

"What's with you guys—you got a problem or somethin'?" one of the boys called out. The others laughed. "Yeah, you got somethin' wrong with your plumbing?" another piped up.

"It's been hours," said Sarah. She hoped they wouldn't send someone with her to the bathroom. She was going to try to use the phone, even though it was risky. But it wasn't clear that these boys were going to let them go without hurting them.

"Oh, go on, go pee!" said the ringleader. "And take your retard with you. Just remember I'm keeping a sharp eye on your friend here. Hurry back!"

Sarah stood up and took Mikey by the hand. Quickly they made their way through the swinging doors into the back of the restaurant. As soon as the doors stopped moving, she crouched down on her haunches and grabbed onto Mikey's arms.

"Listen to me, Mikey, this is important."

Mikey's eyes opened wide and his lips began to quiver. She was scaring him by being so intense. She relaxed her hands and spoke more gently.

"I want to ask you to do something for me, Mikey. It's not hard. I'll be very proud of you. You just have to stand here and be as quiet as a mouse. If anyone comes through the doors, just start shouting 'Sarah.' OK?"

Mikey nodded. "Shout 'Sarah.'"

"Only if someone comes through the doors. Got that, Mikey?"

He nodded again, and watched her make her way toward the back of the corridor. Instead of going into the door marked LADIES, Sarah pushed on the door marked EMPLOYEES ONLY. Inside the kitchen she found what she was looking for—a phone. Quickly she dialed 911. When a voice answered, she said, "Robbery at The Scoop, around the corner from the Century Theater. Six teenage boys, probably unarmed. Come quickly." She hung up and dashed through the door. To be on the safe side, she went into the bathroom and used the toilet. She wouldn't get another chance too soon. Then she heard Mikey yelling her name.

She came running out and found Mikey standing with one of the boys. Her brother was screaming and hitting his head with his balled fists, something he only did when he was very agitated. She crouched down and hugged him until he stopped yelling.

"It's OK, Mikey! I'm very proud of you. You can stop shouting now."

"Come on!" said their companion, pushing the two of them through the swinging doors. "My ice cream's gonna melt."

Sarah could feel her heart pounding in her chest. It was lucky that he hadn't come in two minutes sooner. He might have seen her coming out of the kitchen. What would he have done if he'd found out what she was up to? Hurt them before taking off?

Taken one of them hostage? And how soon before help would arrive? In time or too late?

The answer came a moment later. Through the back and front doors burst a half-dozen police officers, their guns drawn. The six teenage boys dropped to the floor and put their hands behind their heads. The ringleader glanced briefly at Sarah, and then set his face in a mask of defiance.

"OK, you guys, get up and move over to the wall. Let's see if you're packing anything."

While several of the officers frisked the boys for weapons, one of them, a big young black man, questioned Sarah, Latesha, and the two workers behind the counter. Sarah told her that the ringleader was named Ice.

When the officer heard that, he shouted to his companions, "Hey, fellows, looks like we bagged Ice Arnold and the Crypts!"

He walked over to where Ice and the others stood spread-eagled against the wall. He spoke to the back of Ice's head. "OK, Mister Arnold, looks like you really did it this time. You heard what the judge said the last time—one more strike and it's off to juvenile detention. Lucky you guys are still minors or you'd be taking a long ride."

The officer walked back to the four young people at the back table and asked, "You all right? Need a ride somewhere?"

Mikey and Shawna stared at his shiny badge, the big gun in the holster at his side, the dark wooden nightstick. Outside, the red light on the police car flashed red shadows onto the front window in a steady rhythm.

"A ride in a police car!" shouted Mikey. "Give us a ride!"

The officer laughed. "I can see we have two eager customers here. I'd hate to disappoint such loyal fans. Come on."

When the police car pulled up to the Eisenbergs' house a half-hour later, Mr. and Mrs. Eisenberg dashed out to find out what disaster had befallen Mikey now. They were shocked to see their beaming son sitting in the front seat between two burly black officers, wearing a shiny silver badge and holding a nightstick with both hands. Sarah sat in the back, grinning.

"It's OK, Mom, Dad. Just another dull day at the movies. Too bad life can't be as exciting as the silver screen." She laughed at their bewildered expressions. "You always said life with Mikey would turn out to be one hell of an adventure!"

6

A Half-Empty Glass

How many more years will I have to go to Hebrew school? Sarah muttered under her breath as she sat waiting for class to begin on this raw, darkening late November afternoon. Here she was, only five weeks shy of fifteen, but she was still sitting in a synagogue classroom, learning about the Maccabees—just as she had done when she was five years old. Honestly, Jewish education was just endless!

And yet, despite her complaints, Sarah had to admit that there was something reassuring about being here. After all the changes of the past six months—moving from the suburbs into the city, starting a new school, making new friends—it was nice settling into familiar synagogue routines. Even though the Eisenbergs had only joined Temple Beth Shalom right before Rosh Hashanah, she already felt at home there. So much was the same as in her old synagogue—the same prayerbook, many of the same melodies, even the same sweet red wine that was served for Kiddush. Even better, the rabbi at the new synagogue was a dynamic young woman named Avivah Axelrod, who was the exact opposite of stern old Rabbi Rackman. Although she would never admit it to her parents, Sarah actually looked forward to the Friday night sermons—well, to some of them, anyway. And she really enjoyed Rabbi Axelrod's teaching. In fact, confirmation class was often the high point of her week.

"Hey, Sarah!" shouted Zeke, a tall, dark boy sitting in the back of the classroom.

Sarah twisted around to look at him. Zeke was the class clown, a rowdy troublemaker who had managed to make it through the entire Temple Beth Shalom curriculum without learning to read Hebrew or much of anything else. Her new friend Naomi had told Sarah that the only reason Zeke had had a bar mitzvah was because his dad was a vice-president of the synagogue board. Sarah wondered what Zeke could have done for his bar mitzvah without making a total fool of himself.

"What do you want, Zeke?" she fired back when she saw him grinning at her.

"Wanna make Axelrod really mad?"

Sarah snorted and turned back to face the front of the room. No, she did *not* want to make the rabbi mad! Zeke was so incredibly immature, like so many of the fourteen- and fifteen-year-old boys she knew. All they cared about was making trouble and harassing girls. Didn't they ever grow up?

"Whadya say, Eisenberg? How 'bout it?" Zeke was incredibly persistent.

"Oh, get a life, Kassenbaum!" Sarah grumbled. She glanced over at Naomi sitting two desks away. Her friend smiled at her and rolled her eyes toward the ceiling.

Meeting Naomi Cowan was one of the nicest things that had happened to Sarah this year. It had taken Sarah all this time to warm up to the kids in the class. Since the others had been going to Hebrew school together almost their whole life, they had first struck Sarah as cliquey, not interested in a newcomer like her. But when the upper grades of the Hebrew school had gone down to Washington, D.C., last month to visit the Holocaust Museum, she had sat next to Naomi all the way there and back—and had discovered to her surprise that the other girl was actually quite friendly and eager to get to know her. They had arranged to get together once or twice during their winter break.

"What's a' matter, Eisenberg?" Zeke shot back. "Afraid the rabbi will tell your parents if you're naughty?"

"And what precisely *will* the rabbi tell them, Mr. Kassenbaum?"

Rabbi Axelrod stepped into the room from the corridor, wearing her familiar broad grin and white knit kippah that reminded Sarah of a doily. Today she was dressed more casually than usual, in a brightly colored sweater and blue wool skirt.

"Oh, Rabbi Axelrod," whined a small, skinny girl sitting in the front row. "Zeke was planning to do something to make you *really* mad. He was trying to get the rest of us to join him."

"Why don't you go take a long walk off a short pier, Glattstein!" growled Zeke from the back of the room. Sarah, Naomi, and David Levy, a tall, cute boy sitting on the other side of Naomi, all laughed. Even Rabbi Axelrod had to suppress a grin. Rebecca Glattstein and Zeke Kassenbaum were constantly getting on each other's nerves: one was the class devil, and the other, Miss Goody Two-Shoes. A lethal combination.

"Rabbi Axelrod, did you hear what Zeke said to me?!"

The rabbi walked over to the front of her wide gray steel desk and sat down facing the handful of teenagers in the room, her booted legs crossed at the ankles and swinging slowly. She let the silence fill with the steady click-click of heels tapping metal before speaking.

"Why don't we call a truce for now and get on with today's class?" She went on quickly without waiting for a response. "OK, who's here today—Zeke, Rebecca, Naomi, David, Josh, and Alex. Anyone know if Miriam's coming today?"

Six heads shook slowly from side to side. Nobody ever knew if Miriam would show up for class. In fact, nobody knew much of anything about Miriam these days. She had become the class mystery, a locked door. Even Sarah felt like more of an insider than Miriam seemed to be.

On that long bus ride down to Washington, she had asked Naomi about Miriam. Naomi had shrugged her shoulders.

"Beats me what's going on with her. She didn't used to be this way. Until last year, she used to be a lot of fun. She came to my birthday parties, I went to hers. Once in awhile we went to a movie or to the mall. But something happened last year that made her change. Her parents got divorced, and she and her mom moved out to the suburbs. Miriam switched to a new school. I heard that things were really bad before the divorce. Miriam's mom had to call the police a few times because her dad threatened to hurt her. When I asked Miriam what was going on, she bit my head off and told me it was none of my business. So I left her alone. Other kids told me that she was nasty to them, too. I was just trying to help, not be nosy or anything."

"Did Rabbi Axelrod say anything to the class—I mean, about the divorce or about why Miriam wasn't here?"

Naomi shook her head. "No, she just told us to respect Miriam's privacy and not to intrude. Yeah, that's the word she used, 'intrude.'"

Sarah hadn't asked any more questions. But ever since that conversation, she had observed Miriam more closely when she did show up for class. She recognized the sad eyes, the restless doodling, the way Miriam twisted the ends of her hair around her index finger. She knew what Miriam must be feeling. She knew that their lives were very different—Sarah's parents weren't divorced and didn't threaten each other. But things weren't so perfect for Sarah either, not by a long shot. Like Miriam, Sarah sometimes got into what her mother called "black holes," when she felt that the whole world was against her, that nothing was going right. During these periods she would mope around, hiding out in her room for hours, listening to sad songs and writing depressing poems. She imagined that was what Miriam was feeling—but much, much worse from the looks of her.

Rabbi Axelrod glanced down at her watch. "Well, we can't wait any longer."

Sarah looked at the rabbi's face and read concern in her wrinkled forehead, not anger. So Sarah wasn't the only one worried about Miriam.

That night Sarah dialed Miriam's number three times and then hung up each time when someone picked up the receiver. She was very nervous about calling. What would she say if Mrs. Lieber answered the phone? That she was worried about Miriam? How would that sound coming from a fourteen-year-old who hardly even knew Miriam? And what if Miriam herself

answered? "Oh, hi, Miriam, it's Sarah Eisenberg. I was just wondering why you haven't been coming to confirmation class. Is
everything all right?" Miriam would bite her head off for being
so nosy!

Sarah stared at the phone in her hand and debated what to
do. Why was she getting involved in Miriam Lieber's troubles?
She had enough troubles of her own. Although she now had a
few friends at Springfield and Naomi at Beth Shalom, she still
felt like an outsider, a misfit. Life as a teenager was so impossible! How could she help Miriam when she couldn't even help
herself?

But maybe she was managing better than Miriam. When Miriam did bother to show up for confirmation class, she looked
awful. Her hair was wild. She wore nothing but black. And she
always looked so *sad*. Time and again Sarah would glance over
at her and catch her staring off into space, lost in thought or just
lost. Maybe if she helped Miriam by becoming her friend, she
would be helping herself. Maybe if she talked to Miriam and
understood what she was feeling, she wouldn't end up like her.

Summoning up her courage, she again punched in Miriam's
number. The phone rang three times and then someone picked
it up.

"Hello." It was a mature woman's voice. Probably her mother.
Sarah froze. Now what?

"Hello?" repeated the woman on the other end. "Hello?"

"Uh . . . hello," said Sarah. "Can I speak to Miriam?"

"Who is this?" the voice demanded, suspicious—or so it
seemed to Sarah.

"I'm a . . . friend," stammered Sarah, "Sarah Eisenberg. I'm in
Miriam's confirmation class. Can I speak to her?"

"What is this—a conspiracy? First the rabbi calls, and now a classmate. Miriam misses just a few classes because she's not feeling well, and all of a sudden everyone starts hounding her. Why can't you leave us alone!"

"I'm sorry, Mrs. Lieber, really I am," mumbled Sarah, not quite sure what she was apologizing for. "I didn't mean to bother you or Miriam, just to let Miriam know I'm thinking of her. We all are. Tell her we all hope she feels better soon."

After she hung up, Sarah felt foolish. What had she accomplished by calling? She hadn't even gotten to speak to Miriam. Mrs. Lieber probably thought she was a total jerk. She hadn't asked exactly what was wrong with Miriam so she couldn't even bring information back to the others. How dumb to think that Miriam's situation had anything to do with her own!

But the following Tuesday when she saw Miriam sitting in her seat in the last row, Sarah changed her mind about getting involved in Miriam's troubles. She resolved to speak to Miriam after class. Maybe she would invite her to join Naomi and her during winter break, to go shopping with them or catch a movie. She probably needed friends right now.

As soon as class ended at nine, Sarah walked over to Miriam's desk and whispered, "I'm glad you're feeling better."

Miriam looked up from her book, startled. "Who told you I was sick?"

It sounded more like an accusation than a question to Sarah. "Your mother. Didn't she tell you I called last week?"

"Of course not!" snapped Miriam, looking out the window and frowning. "Why would she do a normal thing like that? She believes in protecting me from unnecessary stress."

Sarah was feeling more and more uncomfortable. Why was it so hard to be nice to this girl? Why did she have such an attitude problem? And what was all this stuff about stress?

"Miriam," she tried again, "I don't want to pry, honest, I just want to be your friend."

Miriam looked at Sarah strangely, then turned away to stare out the window again.

Sarah felt color warming her cheeks. "Well, if that's the way you behave when someone tries to be nice to you, Miriam," she said, "it's no wonder you have no friends!"

And without waiting to see Miriam's reaction, Sarah marched out of the classroom and into the chilly December night to wait for her dad to pick her up. She was so angry she didn't even button up her jacket but let the bitter wind lace through her sweater to cool down her hot blood.

Sarah wasn't surprised that Miriam was absent the following Tuesday night. In fact, she was glad. That whole week she had been stewing over the brief exchange the two girls had had at the end of last week's class. What was the matter with Miriam? Was she a snob? Was she just a bitchy type? Was it something Sarah had said, or was she just mad at the world in general? And why was Sarah wasting her time worrying about this? How could she have thought that the two of them had anything in common?

She had thought about calling Rabbi Axelrod to talk about it, but she hadn't really known what to say—so she hadn't said anything. It was really none of her business.

Then the rabbi paired her with Miriam for the Hanukkah project—an oral report about some aspect of the Maccabean revolt.

"Do I have to work with her?" she asked the rabbi, her eyebrows raised above her blue eyes. She looked over at Naomi, who was frowning. "Miriam might not be able to . . . follow through on this."

"Just give it a try, Sarah. If she says no, she says no."

Sarah wouldn't look in Naomi's direction, although she could imagine her friend's disappointment.

"Naomi," Rabbi Axelrod said, "I'd like you to do your report with Zeke."

"Rabbi Axelrod!" Naomi cried. "Have pity on me! You know he'll never follow through."

"Just give it a try, Naomi. You might be surprised. Good luck!"

"You'll need it!" shouted Zeke from his back seat. "And so will Eisenberg!"

"That's for sure," piped up Alex Berg, a wiry boy with a high-pitched voice. "Everyone knows that Miriam Lieber has a screw loose."

"I'm not going to ask you for your source of information, Alex, nor do I want to continue this discussion," said Rabbi Axelrod, a sharp edge to her voice. "You all know where I stand on the subject of rumors and gossip. I'll leave it up to Miriam whether she wants to share any of her private concerns with any or all of us. For now, I'll leave it to Sarah to contact her about her project." Rabbi Axelrod glanced around the room, sensing the tension.

"Now let's get back to the assignments. Who wants to work with Rebecca?" She shot a warning glance at Zeke, started to say something, then thought better of it. "David, how about you?"

Despite the rabbi's glance, Zeke let out a loud laugh, then fell backwards out of his chair. Even the rabbi didn't try to stifle her laugh this time.

When Sarah called Miriam that night, she let the phone ring until someone picked it up. She was surprised to hear a man's voice. She thought the Liebers were divorced. Was this her mom's boyfriend?

"Yes, what is it?"

Sarah thought he sounded upset, tense.

"Uh, this is Sarah Eisenberg. I'm in Miriam's confirmation class. Can I please speak to Miriam?"

"I'm afraid not. She's not . . . available."

"Is she sick again?" Sarah guessed.

"Who told you?" It was more an attack than a question.

"Told me what?"

"That Miriam was in the hospital?"

Sarah sucked in her breath. What should she say now? Should she probe further? Should she say, "I'm sorry to hear that," and hang up? Should she offer to visit? What was the right thing to do under the circumstances? She decided to say nothing.

"Have you spoken to anyone else about this? Mrs. Lieber and I are trying to think of Miriam's feelings. She's feeling very . . . awkward about what's happened. She's worried about what other kids will think. Can I rely on your discretion?"

What in the world was he talking about? What had happened to Miriam? Why was she so sensitive about being sick? Lots of people ended up in the hospital. Why was her father being so melodramatic?

"Mr. Lieber," she said hesitantly. "What exactly *don't* you want me to say to other kids?"

There was a moment of heavy silence. Sarah could hear a sniffle, then a loud sigh. "You say you're a friend of Miriam's?"

"Yes," answered Sarah. She *wanted* to be her friend.

"Well, I suppose she needs a friend right now." Another long pause. "Sarah, isn't that what you said your name was? Well, Sarah, Miriam's in the hospital because she's depressed. She . . . she swallowed some pills and we very nearly lost her." Again Sarah heard the sniffle, louder this time.

"Oh my God . . ." stammered Sarah. "I didn't know."

"Then why did you mention her illness?"

"Miriam said something to me about it. I didn't really understand what she was saying. But I want to be her friend. I want to help."

"There's not much any of us can do to help now. She's in her doctor's hands. We've done all we could. Frankly, we're still in a state of shock. We always thought we were good parents, that despite the divorce we always thought of Miriam's needs first. We never meant to let our troubles hurt her."

"Uh, Mr. Lieber," interrupted Sarah, feeling embarrassed by all these private comments Miriam's father was sharing with her. "Can I visit her?"

"I'm afraid not, Sarah. The Madison Clinic has rules about such things. Only immediate family members are allowed. Sorry. But I do appreciate the gesture."

"Well, then, tell her I'm thinking of her. Ask her to call when she's feeling better."

"I will, Sarah. And thanks for your concern."

She sat with the receiver in her hand for several minutes after Mr. Lieber hung up. She felt like talking to someone about what she had just learned, but she didn't know who. Not her parents—they would get all worried about teenage depression and suicide and blow the whole thing out of proportion. They'd probably start asking her all sorts of questions about herself: Did she ever think about doing something like that? Was she sure she didn't want to see a therapist to work through her feelings? No, they were absolutely not the right ones.

Rabbi Axelrod? No, she didn't know her well enough yet. For that matter, she didn't know anyone well enough yet, not even Naomi. She was too out of touch with her old friends back home, but not well enough connected to her new ones. She wasn't quite ready to trust them with secrets.

No, she would have to talk to Miriam herself. She would go to the Madison Clinic and figure out how to get to see her. It wouldn't be the first time she'd broken a few rules.

The Madison Clinic was not at all what Sarah had expected. When she thought about mental hospitals, she imagined prison-like brick buildings with bars on every window and guards at every door. But the Madison Clinic was nothing like that. It consisted of several low buildings clustered around a magnificent Victorian mansion. Even though it was winter, Sarah could see how beautifully landscaped the grounds were, with trees and bushes everywhere and winding gravel paths connecting the buildings to the main house. She could see tennis courts and a pool beyond the last building. It looked more like a country club than a mental hospital!

She walked up to the front door of the mansion and walked in. She found herself in a wide hallway, facing a circular staircase crowned by a glittering crystal chandelier. Off to one side sat an elderly lady behind a wooden desk, writing in a large ledger.

"Can I help you?" the woman asked, looking up at Sarah.

"I came to visit Miriam Lieber," announced Sarah, trying to sound much more confident than she felt.

"Miriam Lieber? Lieber?" The receptionist brought her pencil to her mouth and then tapped it a few times against her pursed lips. "Oh, yes, the young woman who was admitted last Saturday. Are you a relative?"

"Yes," said Sarah emphatically. "I'm her older sister . . . Sarah."

"I see," said the older woman absent-mindedly. "I don't remember seeing you before. But perhaps you were here on a different shift."

"That's right!" Sarah agreed, too enthusiastically she thought. She told herself to calm down, to act nonchalant. "I came with my parents. But I'm alone today. I took the train and walked from the station."

Why was she talking so much? She sounded nervous. The whole point was to say as little as possible so as not to raise suspicions. What if this woman called the Liebers to check out her story? What if she checked Miriam's records and discovered that she had no sister?

But she needn't have worried. Just then the phone rang, and the receptionist waved her toward one of the low buildings near the parking lot. "The adolescent unit, at the end of the walk. Oh, and I assume you're sixteen. Otherwise . . ."

But Sarah didn't wait for her to finish.

It was so quiet inside the adolescent unit. No crazy screams or people banging on walls. Just the low hum of two vending machines, the murmur of voices in the nurses' station, the muffled sound of a TV in a room somewhere.

Sarah walked up to the young man at the desk and said, "I'm here to see Miriam Lieber."

He smiled up at her. "And who might you be?"

"Sarah. I'm Miriam's sister. Her *older* sister."

No more questions. Sarah began to relax. She was going to pull this off. But the next moment she was filled with dread. What exactly was she doing here? What if Miriam didn't want to see her? What if she gave her away to the staff here? What if she told her it was none of her damn business to stick her nose in here? Maybe she should forget the whole thing.

But it was too late for that now. The young man stood up and came around to the front of the desk. "Come with me, Sarah. Miriam will be glad to see you, I'm sure. By the way, my name's Ned. I'm new here. Just began yesterday."

He led her down a corridor to a set of double doors with small glass windows at the top. From his pocket he took a large ring of keys and unlocked the doors, swinging them forward and walking in. Sarah followed behind, nervous but curious. They walked through a large lounge, filled with round tables at which sat a handful of teenagers, talking quietly, playing cards or board games. Some of them were smoking cigarettes, which surprised

Sarah. In one corner huddled an obese woman in a nurse's uniform, staring at a big TV screen. A few of the teens glanced at Sarah briefly as she walked through, then went back to what they were doing.

Maybe they think I'm being admitted, thought Sarah, horrified. Do I look crazy? Then she realized that they didn't look crazy either. In fact, they looked like normal kids just hanging out. If she hadn't known this was a psychiatric hospital, she would never have pegged them as "disturbed." So why were they here? And how were they any different from her?

"Miriam is still keeping pretty much to herself," whispered Ned over his shoulder. "They tell me that it usually takes them a few days to come out of their shell, especially the ones who are depressed. I bet she'll be out here with the others by the weekend."

He stopped in front of a locked door. Through the large window, Sarah saw Miriam lying on a narrow bed, her hands under her head, staring up at the ceiling. Sarah noticed that there were small wire cages around the overhead light and the outlets. Miriam's black boots sat on the floor next to the bed, minus laces.

"This is the last day she'll be in this room," Ned said. "We take extra precautions with the ones who've tried to hurt themselves. You know, taking away shoelaces, belts, watches, anything they can use to harm themselves. By the way, this is a one-way mirror—she can't see or hear us."

Sarah said nothing to her companion. She was too shocked. How awful to be caged up like this! Why had Miriam done it? Why would anyone want to kill herself at age fourteen? What horrible thing had happened to her to make her want to end her life?

She finally spoke when she saw Ned looking at her, waiting. "Can I speak to her?"

"Sure, but she'll have to come out and talk to you in the lounge. We're still keeping an eye on her, you know."

He slid the key into the lock in the center of the knob and turned it. Miriam started at the sound and sat up. Her eyes opened wide when she saw Sarah.

"Cheer up, Miriam!" Ned boomed out like the host of some stupid TV kids' show. "Your sister's come to keep you company."

Sarah held her breath. The moment of truth. Would Miriam give her away?

"Thanks, Ned," Miriam muttered. "Are you going to lock her up her with me and take away her belt too?"

Ned laughed. "No, I'm not. In fact, why don't the two of you go out to the lounge to talk. It's much nicer than staying in this tiny room."

Miriam shrugged and stood up, pushing roughly past Ned and Sarah. Ned followed behind and motioned Sarah to follow. He left Sarah with Miriam at one of the tables. The others looked over at them but said nothing. There seemed to be unwritten rules here: Respect other people's privacy. Don't ask questions.

"So, Sarah," began Miriam, staring down at her hands. Sarah thought that Miriam's speech was a little slower than usual, but she was afraid to comment on it. "You're my sister, huh? Well, I have to admit I'm glad to have company. It sure gets boring in there."

"Do you want to talk about it, Miriam?" Sarah blurted out. "I mean, I don't know what to say . . . except I'm glad the pills didn't work."

Miriam laughed, but there was no humor in the laugh. It sounded like dry leaves blowing on the sidewalk. "Sure, I'll talk about it. I've already talked to everyone else—the psychiatrist, the social worker, the rabbi . . ."

Sarah's eyes widened. "To Rabbi Axelrod?"

"No, to some rabbi who works here. I didn't mind talking to him because he doesn't know me. I'll probably never see him again once I'm outta here."

Sarah waited for her to continue. Miriam's eyes suddenly filled with tears. She tried to fight them off but a few escaped and trickled down her cheeks. Sarah looked away, embarrassed.

"Hey, would you like a Coke or something?" Sarah said, jumping up. "I've got a ton of change."

Miriam smiled and wiped the corners of her eyes with one wrist. "Sure. Thanks. I'll owe you one."

When Sarah came back to the table with the two cans of soda, Miriam had composed herself. But Sarah noticed that the tough mask had been replaced with softer features. It made Miriam look younger, more fragile.

"OK, Sarah, since you made the trip all the way out here, I figure I owe you a story. You asked me why I did what I did. To tell you the truth, I'm not even so sure now myself. At the time, I told myself I had no choice. My parents are always on my case. They give me no room to breathe. It's bad enough that they got divorced and almost killed each other in the process, but now they want to use me to keep hurting each other. My mom tries to turn me against my dad, and my dad returns the favor. I hate shuttling back and forth between their houses. I don't know where I live anymore. And if I want to change my plans, it's such a big deal! They each blame the other one for making their life difficult. I miss my old friends and my old school. I hate where we live, and I hate pretending that I like things the way they are now! I don't see any way things are going to get better, either. I figured I'd teach them both a lesson by killing myself."

Her voice shook as she came to the end of her speech. Sarah reached out her right hand and placed it on Miriam's, then she pulled it back when Miriam drew hers away.

"I don't know, Sarah. I know that killing myself wouldn't have solved anything, but I couldn't see any other way out. Mom and Dad are so caught up in their private war that they don't seem to care about me anymore."

"Maybe they will now," said Sarah softly. "Your dad seemed really worried when I talked to him."

"He did?" Sarah heard the thrill in Miriam's voice. But it was soon gone, replaced with the hardness that was so familiar to Sarah. "Yeah, well, don't hold your breath. He's worried for now, but he'll go back to his old ways as soon as I'm out of here."

"Maybe not, Miriam. Why don't you give them a chance. And don't give up on yourself."

Sarah was surprised at the passion in her voice. She really meant what she said, but she wondered whether Miriam would believe her.

"Maybe you're right," said Miriam in a voice so low that Sarah had to lean forward to hear her. "I know that my parents care about me. The shrink says that doing what I did was a wake-up call to them. They won't forget about me so easily anymore. They got really scared by what happened." She paused, took a deep breath. "So did I. It was awful having my stomach pumped at the hospital. And I hate being locked up in that little room and watched all day. I won't try anything like that again. I told them that but they won't believe me."

Miriam smiled sadly. "You know, Sarah, I'm really glad you came out here to see me. I guess I've been pretty bitchy to you and everyone else for a long time. I'd like to try to change. I think we could be good friends."

Sarah smiled. "I know we could. I was hoping that maybe you, Naomi, and I could do something over winter break . . . if you're home by then. Go to a movie or the mall or something."

"It's a deal!" said Miriam. "You better believe I'll be out of here by then. I want to be home to collect my Hanukkah presents!"

"Oh, that reminds me!" said Sarah. "We're supposed to do a report together for Rabbi Axelrod. I guess that won't work now, huh?"

Miriam shrugged. "Oh, I don't know about that. If you bring me the stuff, we could talk about it on the phone. I've got lots of free time . . . as you can see."

They both laughed. Sarah looked up to see Ned standing beside her.

"Visiting hours are over for today, girls. Sarah, you'll have to say goodbye to your sister and come back another time."

The two girls hugged. Sarah turned to go. "Promise me you won't tell anyone you saw me here, Sarah," Miriam whispered. "I don't think I could stand everyone knowing where I was. Let's keep it our secret, OK?"

Sarah nodded. There was nothing like a secret to begin a friendship.

7

Privileged Information

It was four o'clock and already getting dark. Sarah sat on her bed watching the ice pelt the crusted snow on her front lawn. It had been a miserable January so far, one ice storm after another, cold winds that sliced right through your skin to the bone, brooding clouds bringing down the night even earlier than usual. Not that she had minded all the snow days, but it was so boring being stuck at home with nothing to do but watch TV and listen to CDs. And what made it even worse was that her mother was stuck at home, too, since most of her clients couldn't make it to her office for their appointments. At this point, the two of them were really getting on each other's nerves, snapping at each other constantly.

Turning away from the frosted window, Sarah stared at the two paperbacks sitting on her desk. The *Iliad* and the *Odyssey*. How she hated those books! They were ruining her life!

She got up from the bed and walked over to the desk. Stretching from her desk to the window sat five ten-gallon tanks holding her eight mice, bought last year when she had seriously considered becoming a vet. (She had only bought three females at the pet store but one had been pregnant—so she now had eight.) Over the summer, she had changed her career plans (now it was either criminologist or zookeeper), but what could she do with the mice? Donate them to a lab for dissection? Feed them to a boa constrictor? Drown them in the toilet? No, she would just have to keep them until they died of natural causes. The pet shop owner had told her they had a two-year life span. She expected them to kick the bucket any day now.

"You think you have it bad," she now said to them, picking up the two paperback books and waving them toward the tanks, "spinning your wheels all day in a glass cage? Well, you're in paradise compared to me! I'd gladly trade places with you in a minute. You should try reading this boring stuff!"

She threw the books down on the desk and flopped into her chair. "Who gives a damn about 'rosy-fingered dawn'? Sounds like some lipstick color. Why are my parents paying so much money to send me to a private school—and always complaining about it!—just so I can be bored to death? Will knowing about some dead Greek guys make me happy in life? Will the story of the Trojan horse help me get along better with people? I mean, get real!"

Such angry speeches to the mice had helped her get through the fall, when her parents had made her sit for hours at her desk, staring at these books as if she could absorb their knowledge by osmosis. She knew that such tactics wouldn't help her now. In another week, she would be sitting with all the other freshmen, taking first-semester finals. In her old public school, they hadn't had term exams. But at Springfield, semester finals were a *major deal,* taken as seriously as SATS or testimony at a murder trial. How you did on these exams had a lot to do with your final grade, and also what your teachers thought about you for the rest of the year.

For Sarah, the English exam meant even more. Her parents had been down on her lately for her "bad attitude" toward school, especially about English. Sarah had never been a super student. Although she knew she was smart, she was not particularly *studious*. She let her interests dictate how much she put into a subject. If she was particularly interested in something, she would read as much as she could about it, would participate in class discussions, would work hard on projects. But if she found the subject boring or incomprehensible, she would just do the minimum—which wasn't always enough according to her parents and teachers.

Unfortunately, right now her parents were really on her case about school. They had been lecturing her regularly about study habits and laziness, warning her that she would have to change her evil ways or she'd never get into a good college. She was only a freshman, for God's sake! She had three more years to get into gear for college. And so what if she didn't get into a good college? She didn't have to be just like her parents and go to Harvard or Princeton. She didn't want their life anyway! Who wanted to go to an office every day or listen to neurotic people whine about their lives? She would do just fine, thank you very much, doing things her own way.

But they were determined to "motivate" her, as they called it. That was just a euphemism for bribery and blackmail. The deal was that she could go on the high school ski trip to Vermont next month if she aced her English final. And if she didn't, she would have to spend her four days off in her dad's office doing boring clerical stuff like filing or preparing mailing labels. She really wanted to go skiing. She had only gone once before, with Diane Zimmerman's family, and she had loved it! She had been terrible at it, of course, but it had been so different from anything her own family ever did. And the Springfield trip was for four days, not just one. They would stay in a chalet, ski all day, and party at night. Dominique had told her that this trip was always the high point of freshman year. If you played your cards right, you could make friends during this trip that could set you up for the rest of your high school career.

Sarah was genuinely worried about the English exam. They had spent most of the first semester reading and discussing Homer's *Iliad* and *Odyssey*. Sarah had hated most of it. The language was impossible to understand, it was so flowery and old-fashioned. And in the *Iliad*, which had taken up over two months, almost nothing ever happened: The Trojans kidnapped a beautiful Greek woman named Helen, then the Greeks chased after them and sat outside the walls of Troy for ten years, fighting every once in awhile. It might have been OK as a short story or a movie, but there was not enough going on for a whole book. In fact, most of the time, the characters just made long speeches about the gods and their honor. Bor-ing!

The *Odyssey* was a little better, but Sarah couldn't keep all the Greek names straight—Polyphemus the Cyclops, Circe the enchantress, the Sirens, the Lotus-eaters, Scylla and Charybdis. And she would never get the spellings right!

Her parents had gotten more than one call from Dr. Snyder, her English teacher, wondering if there was any trouble at home to explain Sarah's poor performance in class. Her papers were "inadequate," Dr. Snyder told them, too short and "demonstrating little analysis." Sarah almost never volunteered in class, the teacher complained, and seemed "insufficiently prepared" in her reading.

Her parents, of course, explained to Dr. Snyder that there was absolutely nothing wrong with Sarah except that she was lazy and had a bad attitude. They assured her that they would work with Sarah to correct both of these problems.

What her parents meant by "working with" Sarah was cutting down her TV time to almost nothing, restricting her weekend activities with friends, rationing her phone calls, and generally being royal pains about everything. Every night they made her sit at her desk with her English books, staring at the pages until her eyes were crossed. It had helped a little to talk to her mice or to go down to the basement to play with her rabbits, guinea pigs, and ferret—but not enough.

Promising herself that she would only rest for a minute, Sarah now laid her head down on her crossed arms and closed her eyes. She listened to the squeak-squeak of the mouse wheels spinning, picturing the Trojan horse being wheeled into the fortified city of Troy, filled with Greeks in its belly, thirsting for blood. The next thing she knew, it was six o'clock and her mother was bellowing her name, calling her to dinner. She sat up, noticing red crease marks on her forearms where the edges of the *Iliad* had pressed into her skin. Sarah hoped the words had pressed into her brain as well, but she wasn't too hopeful.

The next day, Tuesday, was the first sunny day in a long time. Listening to the local weather Sarah was amused to hear the announcer take credit for the change: "I can promise you clear skies and mild temperatures today and tomorrow." Yeah, and I can promise you that chickens lay eggs, Sarah thought. Honestly, people sometimes said the dumbest things!

When she got to school she went straight to her locker to look for the math sheets she'd left there by accident. They were due today, but she hoped the teacher would give them extra time because of the snow day. She couldn't be the only one to have forgotten her homework.

Dominique, whose locker was only two down from Sarah's, dropped her heavy backpack from her shoulder and rubbed her gloved hands together.

"Brrr . . . it's cold out there! I don't know why we don't all move to Florida or southern California. This weather sucks!"

Sarah smiled. Dominique couldn't stand discomfort of any kind. In the fall she complained that it was too windy; in the winter, too cold; in the spring, too nice to be indoors. The way Dominique told it, her hair was always a disaster, her skin a horror, her body obese. Sarah once teased her that if she were granted three wishes, she would probably complain that it wasn't enough and refuse them.

Dominique took off her jacket and hung it in her locker. She pulled off her gloves and tossed them in. Opening her backpack, she threw some of the contents onto the floor of the locker, and slammed the door shut before they tumbled back out. Sarah loaded up her own backpack with the books for her morning classes and hoisted the heavy pack onto her right shoulder.

"Did you review the *Iliad* and the *Odyssey* yesterday?" Sarah asked as they headed toward the stairs.

"Review?" Dominique laughed. "I never read them in the first place."

"What will your parents say when you flunk the final?"

"I won't flunk," Dominique said, and winked at Sarah.

Just then, Wayne Andrews came running down the stairs, juggling an armful of books and his usual doughnuts.

"Watch out," he yelled, as he came toward the two girls.

Dominique jumped out of the way, but Sarah was a few seconds too late. The huge senior barreled into her, knocking her down and showering powdered sugar all over her head.

"Now look what you've done!" said Wayne, frowning. "I paid good money for those doughnuts!"

"Look what *I've* done?" Sarah shot back. "You were the one who ran into me!"

Just then the bell rang, warning all of them that first period was about to start. Picking herself up and running up the stairs two at a time after Dominique, Sarah tried to brush the white powder off her clothes but failed. She had no time to go to the bathroom to clean up. In fact, she dashed into the math room and slid into the only available seat at the front of the room, just as Mrs. Nakamura was starting to explain the geometry problem on the board.

"Let's try to get here on time, Ms. Eisenberg," the teacher said in her squeaky voice. "We have an exam coming up and we have a lot of reviewing to do."

By now everyone was staring at Sarah's head.

"What'd you do, Sarah, look in the mirror and get so scared that your hair turned white?" teased Crystal.

Everyone snickered. Mrs. Nakamura ran her fingernail down the board, prompting squeals and shrieks from the students. She glared at Crystal.

"I believe that we were about to discuss geometry, isn't that right, Ms. Hunter?"

Sarah looked around to see where Dominique was sitting. She saw her sitting in the last row. Dominique winked at Sarah, and then held up a brass key, which she quickly pocketed. What was Dominique up to now?

At the end of class, totally confused by the geometry review, Sarah dashed out into the hall to wait for her friend. As soon as Dominique exited the room, Sarah confronted her, "What's with the key?"

"Remember I told you that I wasn't going to flunk the English exam? Well, this is my magic key. It gives me special powers."

"Cut the crap, Dominique!" Sarah exploded. "What's the key to?"

Dominique edged closer to Sarah and whispered, "This is a copy of the key to the English department office. Chris is going to try to break into the computer system and get a copy of the freshman and sophomore finals. We can all ace the exams."

"What do you mean 'all'?"

"You, me, and Chris," answered Dominique, smiling broadly.

"Do you realize what you're planning to do? If he gets caught, he'll get expelled!"

"Chris is too smart to get caught. This isn't the first time."

Sarah felt her heart beating fast. "I can't do it, Dominique! It's too risky."

"And how do you think you'll do without seeing the test ahead of time?" Dominique retorted. "You told me you weren't prepared. And what about your parents' threat to keep you from going on the freshman ski trip unless you get an A?"

"But stealing the exam!" said Sarah, her voice rising, and then quickly falling when she noticed the stares of other students passing by. "If we get caught, we'll get suspended, and I'll lose a lot more than a ski trip."

"Suit yourself, Sarah," said Dominique, starting to walk toward her next class. "It's your funeral." With a shake of her head, she flung her long brown hair back over her shoulders and laughed.

As she watched her friend walk away, Sarah felt a knot in her stomach and a dryness in her mouth. What should she do now? If she joined in Dominique's scheme, she could get caught and screw up everything. But if she didn't get caught, she'd ace the test and go on the ski trip. On the other hand, if she tried taking the test without Dominique's help, she would probably flunk and ruin her year. Her parents would become absolute jailers. One thing was certain, though—she wouldn't rat on her friend.

But what should she do?

When Sarah walked into the exam room a week later, she found almost every seat already taken. She walked to the front of the room and sat down in the first row, twisting around to see who was sitting nearby. Dominique was in the last row, chewing gum and looking remarkably relaxed. When Sarah caught her eye, Dominique smiled broadly and winked. Sarah clenched her fists and whipped around to face front. Damn that Dominique! She was going to get away with cheating, and Sarah was probably going to fail.

Not that she hadn't tried studying for the test. Realizing that she couldn't possibly read all the chapters she'd skipped during the semester, she'd gone to the bookstore and bought Cliff's Notes. Would that be enough to pass? She'd soon find out.

Dr. Snyder looked up from the test booklets on her desk and scanned the room. When her eyes briefly met Sarah's, they seemed stern, almost angry. Sarah looked down quickly. She knew she was doomed.

"All right, everyone," Dr. Snyder announced, standing up and walking in front of her desk. She picked up the thick stack of bluebooks and test packets. "You will have two hours for this exam. We will take a ten-minute break after one hour so that you can stretch, go to the bathroom, or get a drink. Make sure to write legibly. If I can't read it, you'll get no credit."

Sarah swallowed hard. Even if she did manage to answer some of the questions, Dr. Snyder probably wouldn't be able to decipher her awful handwriting. She should probably take her parents' advice and learn to type so she could take exams in the computer lab, an option Springfield offered kids who couldn't write well.

"I would recommend that you not waste time on questions you know you don't know," continued Dr. Snyder. "Just leave them blank and go on. And make sure to leave yourself plenty of time for the essay portion of the test. It counts for half your grade. And no B.S. I'll take off points if you try to pad."

Sarah felt the pen in her hand becoming slippery as her palms began to sweat. It was a freezing day, but she felt heat burning her face and neck. Steel bands of panic constricted her chest, making it hard to breathe. Her mind went blank. She couldn't remember anything she had studied last night. All those Greek names and places blended into a confusing mush.

"Are you all right, Sarah?" asked Dr. Snyder quietly. Sarah was startled to see her standing only a few feet away.

"Sure," Sarah answered quickly, straightening up in her chair. "I'm fine."

"It's just that you look flushed. I thought maybe you were feeling feverish. There's so much flu going around, you know."

"I'm fine," Sarah repeated. She felt eyes staring at her. Why was Dr. Snyder picking on her? Was she trying to make her more nervous than she already was?

"If you say so."

She was relieved when the teacher moved down the aisle back to her desk. But she felt the panic returning when Dr. Snyder looked at her watch and announced, "Very well, class. You may begin."

Sarah glanced down at the sheet of questions. Twenty identities, twenty multiple-choice. She turned to page 2. Ten true/false questions. Choose two of three essay questions. She read the essay questions first since she was most worried about this part of the test: "Why did the Greeks follow their king to Troy and stay with him for ten years? What does Odysseus learn about himself during his wanderings? Discuss the role of fate in the Greek world. Be specific, giving at least three examples to illustrate your argument."

Oh my God! thought Sarah. I'm sunk. There's no way I can pass this test. Goodbye, ski trip. In fact, goodbye, Springfield School. After I flunk this—and probably my geometry and Spanish exams, too—they'll ask me to leave and go to a less challenging school. And my parents will kill me.

Exams lasted two days, followed by a three-day semester break. The waiting was torture. Sarah bit her fingernails till they bled. Without realizing it, she gobbled down a whole box of chocolate chip cookies while watching TV. She couldn't sleep, and two nights in a row she had terrifying dreams of walking down the crowded school halls stark naked. By the time she returned to school on Tuesday, she had black circles under her eyes and a bad cold.

Although she had considered calling up Dominique to find out the right answers to the English test, she had finally rejected the idea. Why should she give her the satisfaction of saying "I told you so." No, she would tough out the wait—and then deal with the fall-out.

On Tuesday, when she walked into English class and saw the stack of bluebooks sitting on the corner of Dr. Snyder's desk, she felt the adrenalin rushing through her chest like a swarm of angry bees. All morning, as she showered and ate breakfast and walked from the train station to school, she had told herself, "It's going to be all right. I always think I've screwed up and it turns out I haven't really done too bad. I just lack self-confidence, like Uncle Aaron always tells me. Who knows? Maybe I even got an A. Miracles do happen sometimes."

But the sight of that tower of blue exam booklets and the slender black marking book lying next to it quickly overcame her wishful thinking. Sarah knew it was all over.

And for once, her fears were justified. When she sat back down with the bluebook after Dr. Snyder called her name and opened up the inside cover, Sarah felt the blood drain from her face. A big red F. Her nightmare had come true.

Behind her, Dominique let out a high-pitched squeal.

"I can't believe it! An A! I knew I studied hard, but it's hard to believe that I aced it."

Sarah jerked her head around and stared at Dominique, who was waving her test in the air and bouncing in her chair. And Sarah wasn't the only one staring. Everyone else was eyeing Dominique with wonder, envy—and suspicion. Although Dominique was smart, she was by no means the class genius.

Dominique noticed Sarah staring at her, and stopped waving and bouncing. Sarah rapidly considered her options: She could rat on her friend, but that wouldn't change her F and would certainly destroy her friendship with Dominique. She could do it anonymously, but Dominique would figure it out. Who else knew? She could do it anyway and at least get revenge, but it would be a hollow victory. No matter how she sliced it, she'd blown it for herself. Getting back at Dominique couldn't change that.

Sarah turned back and saw Dr. Snyder staring at Dominique too. It must have blown her away to read Dominique's exam. And even if she suspected cheating, she couldn't prove it now. She would have had to catch her in the act. No, Dominique had gotten away with it. And Sarah, with all her admirable moral values, had lost out big time. If crime didn't pay, neither did honesty.

Sarah sat through the rest of class in a daze. When Dr. Snyder called on her, she just mumbled, "I don't know," and was relieved when the teacher let it go at that instead of lecturing her. She didn't hear what Dr. Snyder was telling them about

Shakespeare—they were moving on to *Julius Caesar* next—didn't take notes from the board, didn't write down the homework assignment. She didn't even hear Dr. Snyder call her name as she shuffled out of class when the bell rang. It was only when she felt an arm tugging on her sleeve that she snapped out of her fog.

"Can I talk to you for a moment, Sarah?"

Saying nothing, Sarah turned and walked back into the classroom, stopping at Dr. Snyder's big wooden desk. When the teacher addressed her again, she avoided eye contact, looking instead down at her running shoes. Her nose was running like a leaky faucet and she had no clean tissues. She couldn't use her sleeve, so she kept sucking the mucus in, almost choking on the sickly sweet taste.

"What happened, Sarah?"

Still Sarah kept silent. What am I supposed to say? she thought. That I didn't keep up with the reading and then it was too late to catch up? That I should have listened to you and my parents? That I'm sorry, and I'll try harder next time? There won't be a next time. I'm history around here.

"Sarah, look at me!"

Terrified, Sarah looked up, expecting to see laser beams shooting out of Dr. Snyder's gray eyes. Instead she found concern and understanding.

"Tell me the truth, Sarah."

She couldn't stall any longer. "I just blew it. That's all there is to it."

"Was it because you were ill on the day of the exam? I noticed how flushed your face was. Remember I asked you if you had a fever? I suspected you were coming down with the flu. Looks like you're only now getting over it."

Another option suddenly yawned open before Sarah. Dr. Snyder was giving her a second chance! If she agreed that she had been sick, she could take a retest. She would have to study really hard, but she might pull it off the second time around. She would have to tell a white lie, of course, but that wasn't nearly as bad as cheating. And she couldn't get caught because Dr. Snyder herself was making up the story. Sarah was just going along.

"I guess I should have told you I was sick," Sarah said softly, looking down again at her feet so that Dr. Snyder couldn't see her face. She was a terrible liar. "I thought I was well enough to take the test, but I guess I wasn't. I should have stayed home and taken the test another time."

"You can still do that, Sarah. I'm willing to ignore the F and schedule a retest for you. You understand that it'll be all new questions, but if you know the material, you should do fine."

Sarah looked up, sniffling. "Thank you, Dr. Snyder. I'll do my best."

The teacher smiled and Sarah noticed for the first time that she was actually pretty, with fine features and long black eyelashes framing soft gray eyes. Maybe she wasn't the witch everyone said she was.

Dr. Snyder opened her pocket calendar and flipped through the pages. "Let's see . . . Today is Tuesday. How about Thursday after school?"

Sarah felt the familiar racing in her chest. Two days! Could she possibly learn the stuff so quickly? And even if she wanted to, she couldn't cheat on a make-up exam. Dr. Snyder would probably make it up on her home computer. No, this was going to have to be done the hard way.

"Sure," Sarah answered, trying to sound confident. "I'll be ready."

As she walked to her next class, she kept repeating "two days" to herself as if it were a magical incantation that would rescue her. She knew it wouldn't. Miracles might happen, but not to her.

But to Mr. and Mrs. Eisenberg, miracles *were* happening in their house. Their daughter, who had been allergic to studying and hard work for years, was now spending every waking moment at her desk. When her mother asked Sarah why, she simply shrugged and mumbled, "I guess I'm getting interested in this stuff." Mrs. Eisenberg decided not to push it any further. Miracles had to be taken on faith.

Tuesday and Wednesday nights, Sarah hardly slept. She read the Cliff's Notes from cover to cover. She reviewed the study sheets Dr. Snyder had prepared for the exam until she knew every answer cold. She made flash cards of identity questions and asked her mother to quiz her. She read the key speeches, going through them over and over until she understood what they meant.

And to her surprise, she discovered that she was indeed getting interested in this stuff. But she didn't tell her parents that. She had her pride, after all.

As soon as the bell rang at the end of last period on Thursday, Sarah climbed the stairs to the second-floor English room. Dr.

Snyder was waiting for her. She handed Sarah the test sheets and a blank bluebook.

"You know what to do, Sarah. You have two hours, with a short break if you need it. I'll be here marking papers until you're done." She hesitated and grinned. "Good luck."

Sarah flipped through the test, relieved to find questions she knew she could answer. To her surprise, even the essay questions were OK. They were taken right from the study sheets. Sarah raced through the identities, the true/falses, the multiple-choices, the essays, not stopping for a break. When she looked up at the clock, it read 4:20. She had finished in a little over an hour and a half. It seemed like much less.

"Here, Dr. Snyder," she said, handing her the bluebook. "I'm done."

Dr. Snyder looked up at the clock. "That was quick, Sarah. Are you sure you want to hand this in? Perhaps you should check over your answers. You still have about twenty minutes."

Sarah shook her head. "No, I'm done. I've answered all the questions as well as I can."

"OK. I'll have this back to you tomorrow at the end of class."

Sarah left the room with mixed emotions. On the one hand, she felt light-hearted, giddy, as though her head and lungs were filled with helium. She knew she had done well. She had answered every question, and had written essays filled with good examples. She even felt secure about her spelling.

On the other hand, she was afraid of being too confident. What if she hadn't come up with the right answers to the study questions? What if she was so tired from lack of sleep that she wasn't thinking straight? What if she just wasn't smart enough to get an A, no matter how hard she studied? It was better to be pessimistic than hopeful. That way she wouldn't be disappointed if she failed again—and would be pleasantly surprised if she succeeded. She no longer even cared about the ski trip. She just wanted to pass this time so that she wouldn't be kicked out of Springfield. She didn't want a miracle, just a lucky break.

On Friday she was surprised to find Dominique waiting for her outside the English classroom before class started. The two had hardly spoken to each other since the day the tests were returned. Sarah had decided not to tell Dominique about the F or the retest. Dominique tried to pretend that nothing had happened, but Sarah had given her the cold shoulder. Even if Sarah hadn't ratted on her, their friendship seemed doomed. Sarah would never forgive her friend for making crime pay.

"Hey, Sarah," Dominique called to her as she approached the door. "Can I talk to you a minute?"

Sarah elbowed past her. Dominique reached out and grabbed her sleeve, but Sarah shrugged her arm off and walked into the room, sitting down at the back. When Dominique came in a few moments later, she glanced over at Sarah and then sat down at the opposite end of the room.

Sarah found it hard to focus on *Julius Caesar*. She couldn't quite figure out what she was feeling. Nervous? Excited? Jumpy? She kept looking at Dr. Snyder, trying to read her face, but she couldn't find any clues. It seemed like hours until the bell finally rang.

"Here, Sarah," the teacher said when she handed her the bluebook after the classroom had emptied. "Congratulations."

Sarah stood with the booklet in her hand, afraid to open it. She knew she had passed—why else would the teacher congratulate her?—but by how narrow a margin? Had she gotten a D? a C? Suddenly her prayer simply to pass seemed like a lie. She wanted to do more than just squeak by. She wanted that A!

And when she opened the bluebook, she found herself staring at it. A big red A in Dr. Snyder's beautiful, old-fashioned handwriting. Below it she had written: "This is what you can do when you're feeling well!" No, thought Sarah, this is what I can do when I work for something. As Uncle Aaron always told her: "You get out what you put in."

"Thank you," muttered Sarah, looking up into Dr. Snyder's gray eyes.

"Don't thank me, Sarah. This is your achievement. I just graded the test. You did the work."

She headed for the door, feeling the helium float to her head and fill her whole body. She felt fantastic! She wouldn't even mind if clumsy Red Andrews dumped a whole bucket of powdered sugar on her head at this moment. She would kiss him for it, she was so happy.

"Sarah, can I talk to you a minute?"

It was Dominique, waiting for her outside the room. Sarah stopped in her tracks. Now what did she want?

"I'm sorry about what happened, honest I am. I'm sorry I told you about what Chris and I were planning to do. I should have known you wouldn't want to do it."

Sarah suddenly felt sorry for Dominique. Her friend was certainly smart enough to do well on the test without cheating. Did she really feel good knowing she had stolen her A? Could she possibly feel like Sarah was feeling now—on top of the world?

She knew how mountain climbers must feel, so different from the tourists who take cable cars up the slopes. There was simply no substitute to doing it the hard way.

"It's OK, Dominique," Sarah said, grinning. "I did OK on my own."

"You're not mad at me?"

"Nah, you taught me a valuable lesson."

"Oh, yeah?"

"I learned that miracles can happen, if . . ." she paused, then laughed, "if you work hard enough at them."

Dominique stared at her, puzzled. "Are you feeling OK, Sarah?"

"Sure, I feel great. I've just recovered from the flu and climbed a mountain. I've never felt better!"

Without another word, she took off down the hall at a run, grasping her bluebook in her hand and waving it over her head like a trophy.

8

Too Hot to Handle

Why had she let her mother talk her into coming to this party?

As Sarah stood outside Josh Belzer's front door on this cool April night, she debated whether to ring the doorbell or just turn and run while she still had the chance. She looked around to see if anyone would see her leave. The sidewalks were completely deserted. Sarah wondered whether she should be scared to walk back to the train station now that it was getting dark. She still wasn't too sure of the unwritten rules of city life, where and when it was safe, how to recognize danger signals. The Belzers lived in a modest neighborhood of rowhouses and twins in the Northeast part of the city, a section that was still largely Jewish, according to Uncle Aaron, who had grown up here and still had friends here. But still, the city was full of surprises, many of them very unpleasant.

Before she had time to decide what to do, the door opened and she found herself staring into Josh Belzer's squinty brown eyes, which looked enormous behind his thick tortoise-shell glasses. Sarah was not surprised to see him wearing a tie tonight—dozens of tiny black golf clubs alternating with white golf balls on a green background—and a white shirt, even though this was just an informal home party for their synagogue confirmation class. Once a nerd, always a nerd. She herself was wearing her usual denim skirt and sweater, although to dress up a bit she had put on her silver hamsa earrings from Israel and turquoise studs.

"Hi, Sarah!" Josh said too loudly and enthusiastically. "Glad you could come. I was just checking to see if anyone was wandering around lost out here. All the houses do look the same."

Sarah didn't know what to answer. She looked up and down the block, squinting because of the fading light. Josh was certainly right—the houses *did* all look alike: an endless series of narrow two-story brick structures stuck together like the green plastic houses on a Monopoly board. Each had the same tiny front lawn, divided neatly by a short cement walk and three steps leading up to the front door, framed by black wrought-iron railings. On either side of the front steps stood a few evergreen shrubs, most of them badly in need of a trim. How different this block was from her new neighborhood with its big stone houses and old trees, or her old neighborhood in the suburbs, so spread out and neatly manicured.

"Almost everyone else is here," Josh announced, not waiting for her to speak. "Come on in and join the party. Everyone's having a great time."

He turned and walked into the house. Sarah followed him, not knowing whether to close the door behind her or leave it ajar. She decided to shut it, but Josh didn't seem to care what she did. He was already disappearing through a door to the left of the central hall. Sarah heard heavy metal music blaring through the door. At least Josh had the sense not to play Beethoven or Mozart at a party! Maybe there was hope for him yet.

When she walked down the stairs into the refinished basement, she was startled to find even more signs that Josh was finally joining generation X with the rest of them. The only lights in the room were candles and two strobe lights flashing wildly in the semi-gloom. The air smelled of pizza and garlic bread. Nobody was standing in the open space in the middle of the room or sitting on the two couches lining two of the paneled walls. The half-dozen teenagers who were there were clustered in two knots on either side of the food table at the back wall, girls on one side, boys on the other. Josh was standing by himself at the foot of the stairs, waiting for Sarah to come down. He gazed up at her as she walked down, a big goofy grin on his face.

"What d'ya think? Pretty cool, huh? My sister and her friends set it up. They're seniors, you know. Too bad my sister had other plans tonight. She didn't get to enjoy all her work."

"Sure, Josh, it's great."

Sarah tried to sound cool herself. Could the other kids hear what she and Josh were saying? Was this really a cool set-up—or was it ridiculous, a throwback to the sixties? Sarah was now sorry she hadn't fled back home when she'd still had the chance.

Suddenly someone let out a loud shriek and leapt into the center of the room. It was Zeke. The rhythmic bursts of light from the strobes revealed that he was wearing an absolutely outrageous outfit, even for him. He looked as if he were dressed inside out—he was wearing his boxer shorts and undershirt *out-*

side his jeans and T-shirt! His wiry black hair was sheared close to his skull except for the wild thatch on the top of his head. A large silver skull dangled from one ear.

As everyone stared, Zeke began to gyrate wildly to the music. His tall, lean body writhed like a water snake. Occasionally, sounds erupted from his mouth, odd disturbing sounds halfway between a moan and a howl. Nobody else moved. As the music grew faster, so did Zeke, his arms flailing the air like a windmill in a storm.

"What'd I tell you," Josh shouted into Sarah's ear. "A cool party, huh?"

Sarah nodded and moved away from the stairs toward the food table where the rest of the group was gathered. She kept as close to the walls as she could to avoid bumping into Zeke. In the flashing strobes he seemed to be everywhere at once. When she finally reached the table and found herself standing next to Miriam, she immediately felt better.

"Can you believe that guy?" shouted Miriam, tossing her head in Zeke's direction. "I mean, he's got a great body, but the way he's dancing he looks like he stuck his hand in a light socket or something!"

They both laughed. Even though he was *very* strange, Zeke was well liked by everyone in their class, even Rabbi Axelrod. Not only was he funny and unpredictable but he was also big-hearted. When he made fun of people, he was never malicious. Mostly he made fun of himself, especially of his attention deficits that made school—and life in general—so hard for him.

"You think he notices that he's the only one dancing?" Sarah shouted back. She poked her friend gently in the ribs. "Why don't you go keep him company, Miriam?"

"Are you kidding? There's not enough room on the floor for anyone else!"

Again the girls laughed. Ever since Sarah's visit to Miriam in the hospital after her suicide attempt, the two had become close friends. Naomi had become so jealous that she had dropped Sarah as a friend, and had recently announced that she was dropping out of confirmation class after this party. Sarah had tried to talk to her about it, but Naomi had told her to get lost.

The music abruptly ended but Zeke didn't seem to notice. Moments later the music began again, this time loud and slow. Sarah recognized the song. It was by Soundgarden. The words made absolutely no sense, but she loved the melody and the group's voices. She was so caught up in listening that she didn't notice that Zeke had stopped dancing and was walking toward them.

"Hi, Sarah. Hi, Miriam."

Sarah felt a shiver run up and down her spine. Zeke's voice was strong, like the lead singer of Soundgarden. She wished that he wasn't so weird!

"Hi, Zeke," she said. She felt stupid. She couldn't think of anything else to say, although she desperately wanted Zeke to like her.

But Miriam jumped right in. "So where did you learn to dance like that, Zeke?"

He grinned, his straight white teeth an orthodontist's dream. "Natural talent, I guess. With a little help from my local pharmacist."

He dug his right hand behind the underpants and into his jeans pocket. Then he thrust an open palm toward them. In the dim light Sarah could just make out tiny squares of what looked like cellophane or plastic. She had only seen such things in the movies, but she knew what she was looking at—and she was not pleased.

"These, my beautiful ladies, are divine gifts, manna from heaven, tickets to paradise. I invite you to join me on the most remarkable voyage of your lives."

"What are you talking about, Zeke?" asked Miriam. Sarah noticed that her friend's eyes were gleaming with excitement. Sarah only felt dread.

"Don't tell me you two girls don't know what I have in my hand? I took you to be the sophisticated ones in our class—not like the others."

He laughed and glanced over at the opposite end of the table, where the rest of the boys were gathered around the steaming pizza Josh had just brought down from the kitchen. Their host was trying to divide the large pie precisely into the right number of pieces, carefully planning his cuts by moving the silver wheel of the cutter slowly over the surface without slicing into the cheese. Alex Berg was coaching him despite Josh's loud protests that he didn't need any help.

"We *are* sophisticated, Zeke," retorted Miriam. "It's just that you're not being very clear."

Zeke leaned closer to the two of them so that they found themselves pressed against the smooth wood panels of the wall. "Promise you won't tell?" Miriam nodded. Sarah did not, but Zeke didn't seem to notice. "You are looking at premium quality, top-of-the-line, high-test acid." He paused for effect. "LSD."

Sarah gulped. You didn't have to be too sophisticated to know what that was. For years she'd heard lectures about drugs—from her teachers, her parents, camp counselors, TV shows. It was almost enough to make you want to become a drug addict! But not quite. Sarah knew too many kids who had gotten messed up on drugs to want to ruin her life that way.

But Miriam had a very different reaction than Sarah. Her eyes were shining even more brightly than before. "No kidding, Zeke! Where'd you get it?"

"My little secret, sweetheart. Let's just say that I have a very creative travel agent."

Miriam laughed. Sarah did not. Zeke paid no attention to Sarah's silence. He was totally focused on Miriam now, moving in so close to her that Sarah could barely hear their words.

"How about it, Miriam? Want to go on a pleasure cruise with me?"

"Sure, Zeke," answered Miriam, her voice sounding faraway, dreamy.

Sarah felt panic rising in her throat. "Are you sure you want to do this, Miriam? Maybe you should think about it for awhile. And what about the Belzers? If they find out . . ."

"Chill out, Sarah," said Zeke. "If you don't take a few risks once in awhile, you never really experience life. I promise that I won't let anything bad happen to your friend. Believe me, I know exactly what I'm doing."

Sarah felt trapped. Should she tell Zeke about Miriam's depression and suicide attempt? Taking hallucinogenic drugs could be disastrous for her. Should she take Miriam aside and warn her? What about the medication that Miriam was now taking for depression—how would the two chemicals mix? Maybe she should tell the Belzers; but they might call the police and get them all in trouble, especially Zeke. He wasn't a bad kid, just a little wild. What should she do?

She didn't have time to decide. Zeke now grabbed a large bottle of Coke from the table and poured it into two cups. He handed one to Miriam and held his up.

"Cheers!" he said, and then he swallowed one of the small squares in his hand, washing it down with the Coke. Miriam gingerly picked up another of the thin squares of cellophane, hesitated for a moment, and then swallowed it, drinking her soda so fast that she choked. Sarah patted her on the back, muttering, "It's OK, Miriam. It's going to be OK." She knew she was talking to herself.

For the next hour, nothing happened. Sarah tried not to stare at Miriam, but she found herself watching her every moment she could. Miriam and Zeke danced together almost the whole time, and Zeke even seemed to be calming down. Sarah began to tell herself that Zeke had been faking, just trying to impress Miriam.

She walked over to the couch where Naomi and Rebecca were sitting at opposite ends, not talking, watching Zeke and Miriam dance. The boys were still glued to the food table—and each other.

"Well, what do you think?" Sarah said, sitting down between them. "Think they're a number?"

"Who cares?" snapped Naomi, not looking at Sarah, still staring at the two young people holding each other tightly as they shuffled to a slow song. "They probably deserve each other."

"What's that supposed to mean?"

"They're both loosely hinged," replied Naomi, snorting. "One's manic and the other's depressed. They'll make a perfect couple."

"That's not nice!" said Rebecca, turning to face the other two girls. Her mouth was pursed in its customary pout.

"Oh, get a life, Glattstein!" snapped Naomi. "Niceness went out with typewriters and black-and-white TV!"

""Why don't you two cut it out!" shouted Sarah, jumping up from the couch. "It's a party, for heaven's sake. You're supposed to have fun!"

Just then the song ended, and silence fell over the room like a dense fog. The quiet was punctuated by Miriam's voice, terrified, panicky.

"Make it stop, Zeke! I don't want to do this! I've changed my mind. It's all a mistake!"

All eyes focused on the couple standing absolutely still in the center of the room. Zeke was holding Miriam by the shoulders.

"It's OK, Miriam," he said sternly. "I'm here. I'll make sure nothing bad happens to you. Trust me."

Then the music began again, a loud, throbbing beat pounding at the eardrums. Zeke and Miriam began to dance again, Miriam moving slowly, out of sync with the hectic music, Zeke returning to his frenzied movements.

Sarah decided that she had to do something to help her friend. But what? How would Zeke react if she interfered? How would Miriam?

She walked toward the center of the room and tapped Miriam from behind on the shoulder. The other girl turned to face her. Her face shocked Sarah. She seemed almost hypnotized, her eyes staring blankly into the darkness. Sarah tried to make eye contact but failed.

"Miriam!" she shouted. "Miriam! Can you hear me? Are you all right?"

Miriam ignored her and kept dancing. Zeke noticed Sarah and waved her away with one hand. He grabbed Miriam by the hands and began to dance her wildly around the room, faster and faster, until they crashed into an end-table, sending a burning candle flying through the air. It landed on the couch where Naomi and Rebecca sat. Instantly, the fabric burst into flames. The two girls leapt up and began to scream.

Then all hell broke loose. Screaming and running blindly in the dim light, the seven teenagers dashed for the stairs, pulling at each other in panic as they tried to escape the flames and smoke. Seconds later, they were out the front door and into the street, with Josh's parents on their heels. Minutes later, the police and fire trucks arrived, along with a crowd of curiosity-seekers.

Within a half-hour, the fire was out and most of the crowd had gone back to their Saturday night TV shows, leaving only the confirmation class students, the Belzers, a few fire department officials, and the police in the deserted street.

"Well, who wants to tell me what happened?" asked the police sergeant, pulling out his pad and pen. "Let's start with names."

Sarah suddenly realized that Zeke and Miriam had disappeared. She looked around, trying not to attract the officer's attention. Where could they have gone? The firefighters had not found any bodies—thank God!—in the house, so they must have gotten out. But where did they go?

Then something caught her eye, halfway down the block and across the street. In the light of the street lamp, it looked as though a tree trunk had sprouted a cancerous growth on one side, but Sarah knew that it was them.

Quietly, she inched toward the spot, grateful that Josh and Rebecca were bending the police sergeant's ear and diverting his attention. After what seemed like hours, she reached the tree. Sure enough, Zeke and Miriam were the mysterious bulge she had seen. They stood locked in each other's arms, holding on for dear life.

"Are you guys OK?" she asked softly.

"It's the end of the world!" cried Zeke. "The fire to end all fires!"

Sarah was alarmed by the desperation in his voice. Miriam seemed to be, too, although it wasn't clear to Sarah whether it was Zeke's tone or what he said that frightened her. The next moment answered her question.

"Save us, Sarah!" shouted Miriam. "We're all going to die! It's the end!"

Sarah thought quickly. If she brought them back to the police, they would give themselves away immediately and get arrested. And if they disappeared, the police would come looking for them. Then she had an idea.

"Stay here," she told them. "Don't move. It's your only chance."

Zeke and Miriam held each other more tightly, and huddled fearfully against the tree. Sarah ran back to the Belzers' house, where Josh was still holding forth, telling the police sergeant what had happened in excruciating detail.

"You say it was an accident?" the sergeant interrupted Josh. "Who was responsible?"

So there was still time! Sarah took a deep breath and cut Josh off before he could answer the question.

"I'm afraid I am, officer," she said. "It was pretty dark downstairs and I'm sort of clumsy, and I guess I just knocked over the candle by accident."

"That's not true, Sarah!" Naomi protested. "It was Zeke and Miriam—they were dancing so wildly that they knocked the candle off the table!"

"How could you see from where you were sitting, Naomi?" countered Sarah. "It was so dark you could hardly see anything. That's how I knocked the candle over."

"Zeke and Miriam, you say," interrupted the policeman. "How come you didn't give me their names? Where are they now?"

"Uh . . . they left the party just before the fire," Sarah said quickly. "They were . . . you know, eager to be alone. I assume they left the house and took the train somewhere. It's just like them not to say goodbye or tell anyone where they're going. They're both airheads." She forced a laugh.

She looked over at Naomi, who looked at her suspiciously. Please, Naomi, prayed Sarah, don't ruin things! Just keep quiet and I'll explain everything—later. I'll even drop Miriam as a friend, and we can be friends just like we were before. Just don't say another word.

Whether it was Sarah's prayer or her own doubts about what had actually happened, Naomi said nothing more. The police sergeant asked a few more questions, took down their phone numbers and addresses, and left. One of the Belzers' neighbors volunteered to drive the four remaining teenagers home while the Belzers drove to a nearby hotel for the night. Sarah lied and told the neighbor that her aunt and uncle lived nearby. She would walk there and stay over. Fortunately, he didn't make a fuss and insist on driving her.

She walked briskly to the corner and then stealthily made her way back to the tree where Zeke and Miriam still huddled together.

"OK, you're safe now."

Neither of them moved. Sarah felt anger mixing with her earlier feelings of nervousness and fear.

"I hope you're proud of yourself, Zeke," she barked at him, "persuading Miriam to risk her life—and everyone else's—so that you could show how cool you are!"

"Please, don't hurt me," whimpered Zeke. "I'll tell you everything. Only don't hurt me!"

Sarah realized that this was not the time to reason with either of them. That would have to wait. The first priority now was to get them home safely and to keep the lid on their secret.

"Let's go," she said in a gentle voice. "No one's going to hurt you. We're going home."

It took them almost an hour to reach the Thirtieth Street train station, where they could spend the night in warmth and safety. Sarah had quickly rejected the idea of trying to go to either Miriam's or Zeke's house, since they lived in the suburbs, and anyway, they were in no condition to face their parents. And her own parents would probably see through any story she made up. So she had led Miriam and Zeke to the nearest pay phone and called their parents, telling them about the fire and

embroidering her lie about staying with her aunt and uncle—
now they were putting up not only their niece but Zeke and
Miriam as well. She hung up quickly before the parents asked to
speak to their children or for her aunt and uncle's phone number. The story she told her own parents was slightly different,
since they knew very well that she didn't have an aunt and
uncle in Josh's neighborhood. She claimed, instead, that she was
staying with Miriam's aunt and uncle, and said she would take a
train home in the morning. She hated hanging up on them so
abruptly, but she had no choice.

When the three teenagers got to the station, it was almost
deserted. Sarah sat her two companions down on a long wooden
bench and made them promise not to talk to anyone or wander
away. Then she ran to the McDonald's and ordered hot chocolate and fries for all of them. When the other two showed no
interest in the food, she ate their portions as well as hers. Eating
always soothed her nerves.

By then it was midnight. For the next six hours, Sarah dozed
on and off as her two friends talked to her, each other, and
themselves. She tried her best to stay up, both to keep them
company and to keep an eye on them, but she kept falling
asleep. When she woke, they were often still talking, but it
didn't seem to matter whether she listened or not. When she
realized that, she fell back to sleep with a clear conscience and
didn't awake until the overnight train from Boston came in and
the vast central hall filled up with noise and commotion.

At first she didn't know where she was. Looking up, she saw
the brightly colored squares of the ceiling one hundred feet
above her and thought she was dreaming. Then she remem-
bered everything and shuddered. She sat up quickly and was

relieved to find Miriam sitting next to her, crying softly—but still there.

But where was Zeke? Then she spotted him kneeling on the floor surrounded by pigeons. He was feeding them crumbs from a hamburger roll he'd found and talking to them. Luckily, no one paid much attention to him, especially considering the outfit he was wearing. City train stations were filled with weirdos like Zeke.

"Miriam," said Sarah, gently touching her friend on the arm. "How are you feeling?"

"I'm almost myself again," whispered Miriam, wiping a few tears from her cheeks. "Oh, Sarah, that was so horrible! I've never been so scared in my life!"

"I'm glad you're OK now," said Sarah. "When you're feeling better, we can talk about what it was like. It could have been much worse."

"No, it couldn't have been," answered Miriam. "I thought I was going to die. Even though I tried to kill myself before, I didn't really want to die. I was just getting even with my parents. But this time I thought I was doomed for sure, and I was more scared than I've ever been in my life."

Zeke heard them talking and looked up, beaming at them with an impish grin. "Hey, you two, come meet my feathered friends. They're incredible!"

"I think we've had enough of this, Zeke," snapped Sarah.

"Oh, come on, Sarah, I'm still flying. Don't be such a downer. This is child's play."

"Zeke, I've just about had it with you! It's time to pick up your toys and go home. Don't you realize that Miriam could have died last night! Maybe you can tolerate this stuff, even enjoy it, but some people can't. And who knows what damage you're doing to yourself? I have half a mind to turn you in."

Zeke's smile vanished and was replaced by the wide eyes of terror. He came rushing up to Sarah. In the morning light, she saw that his pupils were shriveled to a tiny dot within the large blue irises. She looked at Miriam's eyes. Her pupils were smaller than usual, but not as tiny as Zeke's.

"Don't do that, Sarah, please. They'll kill me!"

"I was just kidding, Zeke," she said gently. "Relax. No one's going to hurt you. I told you that last night."

Zeke's shoulders slumped and he sat down on the other side of Sarah. She glanced up at the clock. Six-fifteen. As soon as she was sure that the effects of the drug had worn off, she would send them on their way and go home. She needed a hot shower, a soft bed, and about twenty hours of TV.

When she walked into her house at ten o'clock, her parents pounced on her and pumped her for every detail she could think of. She told them the same story she had told the police—and then retold it until they were satisfied. Finally they let her go upstairs to shower and sleep. When she came downstairs a few hours later, she went looking for the morning paper.

She was relieved not to find the story of the fire on the front page. But she was disappointed it hadn't even made the first page of the Metro section. She finally found the article on page 16 of the Metro section. It was short and unexciting:

Last night a small blaze broke out in the home of Irene and Samuel Belzer in the city's Northeast section. Apparently the fire started when a candle was accidentally overturned at a party hosted by their son. No injuries were reported. Although the fire was contained to one room, more extensive damage was reported from smoke and fumes.

That was it. No suspicion of arson. No report of missing persons. No mention of any of their names. They were safe.

But the story was not over yet. Miriam had certainly been frightened enough by this experience to avoid drugs in the future, but what about Zeke? From the way he'd been talking, it sounded as though he took drugs often. And he seemed so casual about it, as if there were no danger, no risk. She liked Zeke too much to turn her back on him as though she didn't care. But how could she help him without getting him into trouble? She had promised not to hurt him.

For the next few days she struggled for an answer. At the next confirmation class, Zeke thanked her for "covering his tail," as he put it, but he wouldn't listen to her when she tried to talk him into stopping drugs. Miriam, too, tried to talk to him, but he laughed her off, calling her "gun shy" and urging her to give LSD another chance. He swore that he had been transformed by his experiences with hallucinogenic drugs.

Finally, Sarah made up her mind to act. On her computer, she carefully composed a note to Rabbi Axelrod, keeping it anonymous so she wouldn't have to tell more than she wanted to. There was such a thin line between intervention and betrayal.

The note simply read: "Dear Rabbi Axelrod, I thought you'd want to know that Zeke Kassenbaum is in trouble and could use your help. He may not be ready for it, but I think you could change his mind if you show him you care. Signed, A friend."

Sarah wondered whether she should have mentioned drugs, but decided it was too risky for Zeke. Maybe rabbis were obliged by law to report such things to the police. Maybe Rabbi Axelrod would not feel qualified to handle it herself. But Sarah was convinced that only Rabbi Axelrod could get through to Zeke at this point. He liked and trusted her. And she liked him.

Sarah mailed the letter from center city the next day on her way to school. That night, when she went to bed, she found herself feeling lighter, as though she had shed forty pounds. She knew she had done the right thing. What good was loyalty if it meant letting friends hurt themselves? What were friends for? No matter what happened to Zeke now, she knew she had done the only thing a friend could do. She knew he'd do the same for her.

9

Not So Friendly Persuasion

Only twelve more days until the end of school!

On this warm June morning, Sarah stood outside the thick glass doors of Springfield School, so charged with energy that she couldn't keep her feet still. Before pushing open the doors, she sucked in the fresh spring air, then blew it out through pursed lips. She could hardly wait for the school year to be over. Not that she had such an exciting summer ahead of her—first, a family trip to Williamsburg and Busch Gardens, then six weeks volunteering at the zoo combined with a part-time job as a mother's helper—but anything was better than school!

As she walked down the crowded hallway toward her locker, Sarah played back the past nine months in her memory. What a year it had been! A new school, new friends, a new city. And so many new problems. Despite the good times, she was definitely glad that freshman year was finally over. Next year she would no longer be the "new kid." No longer would she be at the bottom of the pecking order. She would be able to enjoy high school a bit more, even pick on the new freshmen come September.

Reaching her locker, she patiently worked on her lock until it clicked open. No matter how many times she practiced, she still missed the right combination about half the time. One more thing she wasn't good at. She glanced at the calendar taped on the inside of the locker door. Since the beginning of school, she had systematically crossed off each day with a black felt-tip marker. Only twelve squares remained unmarked.

Freshman year isn't over yet, she told herself glumly. There's still one more major hurdle to clear: the freshman prom.

Months ago Sarah had resigned herself to not going. The truth was (although she couldn't admit this to *anyone*) that she didn't really want to go. She hated dances, especially big ones like the Springfield freshman prom. You were expected to dress up, eat a fancy dinner, dance for hours, and then head down to the shore for the grand finale—a barbecue on the beach. And because of keeping kosher she wouldn't be able to eat the meat!

And that wasn't the worst of it. In addition to the "official" program, many kids added a few of their own activities to the schedule: drinking beer, skinny dipping—and having sex. To hear this year's sophomores talk about it, you'd think that the junior and senior proms were let-downs after the ninth graders' bash.

Hearing about the prom from her classmates, Sarah had made up her mind that she had absolutely no interest in going. But she might not have a choice anymore. She and Latesha had made a secret agreement with each other months ago: either they both would go to the prom—or neither would go. Until last Friday, neither of them had a date, which suited Sarah just fine.

They had made plans to go to a movie on prom night. They had told each other that they would have a much better time than the rest of the class.

But then Latesha had been asked to the prom by Tony Parker, and she'd agreed to go, and suddenly everything was different. For the past week, Latesha had been teasing Sarah every chance she could, daring her to ask a boy to the prom so they could go together. Sarah had tried talking Latesha out of going—but it wasn't really fair to her friend. But what could Sarah do about a date? The prom was only six days away!

"Hi, Sarah!"

Dominique Rosenblatt dropped her heavy bookbag with a loud thud in front of her locker. With an experienced twist, she spun her combination lock to the right, then left, then right again, and yanked the narrow metal door open, spilling out several books, a large bag of sour-cream-and-onion chips, a few cans of Diet Coke, and an umbrella.

"Why can't they give us decent-sized lockers?" she whined. "I'm so tired of this happening every day!"

Sarah laughed. Dominique had complained about the size of her locker all year, but she kept cramming more and more stuff into it, never bothering to empty it out. Sarah and Latesha were always teasing her about it, which made her even madder.

Stooping to pick up the mess on the floor, Dominique twisted her head to speak to Sarah.

"So—got a date yet?"

Sarah gulped and stuck her head into her own locker. Why did everyone have to rub it in? Just because Chris had asked Dominique to the prom back in April, she was now lording it over everyone. Every time she bought something for the occasion—a dress, shoes, a bathing suit, earrings—she told everyone about it. Sarah had finally told her to keep the gory details to herself. For a day or two, Dominique had sulked, but then had started up again. Sarah had done her best to ignore her.

And now even Latesha had a date! Maybe Sarah could fake mono or break a leg or figure out some other way to skip the last two weeks of school. It would be torture having to see her two friends every day—not to mention the rest of the class. Sarah was sure she was the *only one* not going to the prom.

Latesha now sauntered up to her locker across the hall from the two other girls. Her bookbag looked considerably less stuffed than Dominique's, probably because she had done most of her homework in study hall on Friday. Latesha was as organized as Dominique was scatterbrained. Sarah fit somewhere in between.

"Well, Sarah, get any phone calls over the weekend?" Latesha asked as she sorted through the books for her morning classes.

"What is it with you guys?" Sarah snapped at her. "You're acting as though the whole world revolves around this stupid dance! I've got better things to do."

Latesha laughed. "OK, OK, you don't need to bite my head off. I can tell by your response that the answer is no."

Dominique straightened up and quickly slammed her locker shut. "It's OK, Sarah, there's always the junior and senior proms. Maybe you'll be a little less shy around boys by then."

"Why don't you go suck eggs, Dominique!" yelled Sarah, slamming her locker with such violence that it sprang back open, banging noisily against the neighboring locker. Books, pens, and spiral notebooks clattered to the floor.

Sarah felt tears welling up in her eyes. These two were supposed to be her friends! Why were they torturing her like this?

Was it her fault that no one had asked her to the prom? Had she sent out a message to the whole freshman class: "Don't date Sarah Eisenberg. You'll be sorry if you do"?

She stooped down and shoveled up the mess at her feet, stuffing the books, pens, and notebooks back into her locker and quickly slamming the door shut. She snapped the lock closed and then started walking rapidly toward her first-period class, not looking back to see how the other two had reacted to her outburst. By the time she reached biology class, she had made up her mind: She would get a date for the prom, come hell or high water. Otherwise, she could never make it three more years at Springfield.

For the rest of the day, Sarah wracked her brain to come up with a plan. In the back of her English notebook, she listed all the boys in the ninth grade, rating them from one to five depending on what she thought of them. Most of them received only a four or a five ("subhuman" or "below subhuman"), but she managed to identify three boys who merited a three ("human"), a two ("acceptable"), or a one ("desirable"). Unfortunately, when she discreetly asked around about them, she discovered that she was not alone in her judgment. Numbers three and two had already been nailed down by Christine and Julia. Rumor had it that number one—Gregory Armstrong—was trying to persuade Crystal Hunter to "uninvite" the senior she'd asked and go with him instead. Fat chance Sarah would have competing with Crystal!

So, what could she do? She could lower her standards and ask one of the subhuman boys—but she'd rather transfer schools than spend twelve miserable hours with one of them.

Then she had a brainstorm. Why not ask a boy from her con-firmation class at Beth Shalom? No one at Springfield would know him, so there would be no danger of gossip afterwards. Even if he was a total washout as a date, no one would ever know. It would be like renting a tuxedo. She could return it after one night without making a major investment.

And the fact that she would be going with a Jewish boy would make it easier for her at home. Her parents had laid down the law about dating non-Jews. "Now that we live in a city where lots of Jews live," her mother had lectured her several times, "there is no reason you can't find one of them to date." She decided not to answer back that most of the Jewish boys she knew were total jerks.

But that didn't matter for once. The point was to go to the prom and not have her reputation ruined. Who could she ask who would be bearable for a whole night?

She quickly ran down the list: Zeke? No way. Too crazy. Even though he'd been getting help with his drug habit after talking with Rabbi Axelrod and a therapist, he was still a wild card. Too risky.

Josh Belzer? No way! He would talk her to death by midnight.

Alex Berg? No, too much of a know-it-all. He would definitely get on her nerves, and besides, his voice was like fingernails on a blackboard. She'd never survive a date with him.

That left David Levy. She hadn't quite made up her mind about David. He was actually cute—tall, with brown hair in a mushroom cut, green eyes, and no pimples. He seemed pretty normal, at least compared to the other fifteen-year-old boys she knew, but you could never tell how boys would behave outside of class. Still, he was worth a chance. And anyway, she had no other options.

Tomorrow night, right after confirmation class, she would ask him. It would be the last time the class met that year. She didn't even let herself consider the possibility that he might say no. It was hard enough imagining what she would do if he said yes.

"Well, what do you want to talk about during our last session?" asked Rabbi Axelrod as the seven teenagers gathered in the small synagogue social lounge the following night. "It's your call."

"How about sex?" asked Zeke.

The others groaned.

"You've got sex on the brain, Kassenbaum," said Naomi. "Why don't you ask your doctor what's wrong with you."

"I'm just a healthy adolescent, Naomi. I'm sure my doctor would agree with me. It's you who've got problems. You know, most doctors warn that virginity is a fatal disease if not treated soon enough."

"That's enough, Zeke," warned the rabbi. Sarah noticed that the corners of her mouth were slightly turned up. "Any other suggestions? I don't hear a lot of enthusiasm for Zeke's idea."

"How about the limitations of Jewish law, especially in modern times?" said Alex.

Again there was a chorus of groans. No one liked Alex's suggestions—except Alex. He was always telling the others that he liked to challenge himself intellectually, and they were always telling him that he was already challenged in other ways, especially socially. Rabbi Axelrod had learned to be quite diplomatic in refereeing such exchanges.

"Other suggestions?" she asked now, acting quickly to head off the usual volley of insults.

"I say we discuss the dangers of interdating."

This suggestion came from Rebecca, whose whiny voice irritated the others even more than Alex's. They didn't even bother to groan this time. They had learned to ignore Rebecca's ideas completely.

"What about talking about next year's class?" offered David. "I mean, some of the things we did this year worked; some didn't. If we talk about it now, maybe we can come up with some good topics for next year."

Sarah listened approvingly to David's comments. They were sensible, unlike the others'. He was neither a nerd nor a jerk. In fact, she liked his suggestion. She had been thinking the same thing, only she was too shy to suggest it. They probably had a lot in common. Yes, he would do just fine for her plan.

But when class ended an hour later after a lively discussion about next year's curriculum, she felt too nervous to put her plan into action. Waiting for her ride just inside the synagogue doors with the rest of the class, she glanced out of the corner of her eye at David, who was peering through the glass doors into the dark night. She only had a few minutes left before one of them was picked up. But how should she open the conversation?

As if by a miracle, David gave her that opening.

"You know, Sarah," he said, when they were the only two left in the hallway, "I'm going to miss you this summer. I kind of enjoyed hanging out with you on Tuesday nights." He laughed softly. "I think we're the only normal ones in the class."

She laughed, too, although her nervousness turned the laugh into a squeaky giggle.

"It's funny you should say that, David," she said. Her heart was racing very fast now, and she found it hard to breathe. "I was just thinking the same thing myself. In fact, I was wondering whether you would like to come to my freshman prom with me. I mean, if you're free next Saturday night."

There, she'd said it! She felt a mixture of relief and anxiety. What would he answer?

For a few moments, he said nothing. Then he spoke, not looking at her, addressing the blackness outside. "I . . . I don't know. I mean, I think I'm free. What do I have to wear? I mean, is it formal or what? Where is it? I mean, oh, here's my mom. Hey, I'll call you later tonight, OK?"

And then he was gone.

When Sarah's dad pulled up moments later, he had to honk several times to get her attention. And she was unnaturally silent all the way home.

Sarah sat near the phone that night and the next, but David didn't call. She debated whether to call him but decided that it was his move now. If he didn't want to go, he should be mature enough to tell her. If not, well, she wouldn't want to go to the prom with him anyway.

Just when she was about to give up, he called. It was already 10:45 on Thursday night. The prom was only two nights away! She decided not to disguise her annoyance.

"Nothing like waiting till the last minute to call, David!"

There was a long pause, then in a quiet voice, David said, "I'm sorry, Sarah, really I am, but . . . I'm really terribly shy and I didn't have the nerve to call till now."

Sarah felt her anger melting. It took a lot of guts to admit being shy, especially for a boy. She herself tried to hide her own shyness from others. Two more points for David.

"That's OK, David," she told him. "It's just that proms take planning . . . that is, if you're coming with me."

She held her breath. Why was this stuff so hard? It was like some complicated dance but each dancer only knew half the steps. If you didn't watch your feet, you'd step on your partner's toes.

"Uh . . . I'd like to go with you, Sarah, I mean, if the offer's still open."

Sarah's heart skipped a beat! Yes! She could call Latesha and tell her the deal was on—they would both be going to the prom. But the next moment her heart sank. What would she wear? There wasn't time to go shopping for a whole new outfit. Tomorrow night was Shabbat, and as soon as Shabbat ended, the prom would begin. She'd have to make do with what she already owned, as pathetic as that was. Maybe David didn't notice such things. As for her schoolmates, well, they knew she always dressed like a slob anyway.

As if reading her thoughts, David now asked, "What do I have to wear?"

"Most of the boys are renting tuxedos but you'll be fine in a suit and nice tie. You have one, don't you?"

"Luckily, I do. We had a family wedding this December, and I got a new suit. I'll borrow a tie from my dad." Another long pause. "How are we going to get there, Sarah? You want to pick me up, or should we pick you up?"

Sarah panicked. She hadn't thought about this detail. Since no one in ninth grade could drive yet, they all had to be driven by parents. Some of the wealthier kids were renting stretch limos, but her parents would never agree to that for a *freshman* prom. She'd be lucky if they'd spring for something like that for her senior prom.

"Why don't you ask your dad to pick me up," she suggested. "It's on your way into town. About eight?"

"Fine. See you around eight."

And then he hung up. Sarah stared at the dead phone in her hand as if it could still speak to her. At last, she set it down, but still didn't get up from the den couch. Was this really happening to her? Was she finally going to join the human race—at least, the adolescent race? Did David actually *want* to go to the prom with her?

She'd find out one way or the other on Saturday night. In the meantime, she'd better take a serious look at her wardrobe. She hoped it wasn't as much of a disaster as she thought.

The night of the prom was perfect. There was a full moon, and the sky was crystal clear. Even though the bright moon and city lights washed out most of the stars, Sarah still could see some sparkling in the velvet sky. She pressed her face against the living room window and peered out, looking for a car slowing down near her house. It was early, but she still wasn't convinced that David would actually show up. He had not called again since Thursday night. Maybe she had dreamed up the whole thing.

But fifteen minutes later, a car pulled up into her driveway and a tall, thin teenager started walking toward her house. Sarah pulled back from the window and ran into the kitchen, where her parents sat over tea arguing.

"I still say the President had it coming," her mother was saying. "He was warned not to be so stubborn on this bill, but he just won't listen."

"It's not his fault that the Congress is so partisan," retorted her father. "They're so damned concerned about the November elections that they . . ."

"Mom! Dad!" Sarah shouted, startling them both. "He's here! What do I do?"

"I'd suggest that you open the door and let him in," answered Mrs. Eisenberg, smiling. "I'd like to meet the gallant knight who's taking my daughter away."

Sarah groaned. Honestly, her mother was *so* corny!

The doorbell rang, and Sarah dashed to answer it. When she opened the door, she was awed by what she saw. David looked unbelievably handsome in his dark blue suit and striped tie. His brown hair was slicked down—except for a stray hair that had escaped his comb. His smooth skin was scrubbed clean and shining.

He smiled at her. "You look nice, Sarah."

She looked down at her dress as if to see who he was talking about. Her simple green dress, loosely gathered at the waist and flaring out at the knees and elbows, flattered her somewhat lumpy figure. The beautiful jade necklace and earrings her mother had lent her made the outfit seem sophisticated. On her feet she wore new green suede shoes with low heels. She and her mother had dashed out to buy them the second she'd come home from school yesterday. Her short brown hair was sleek and glossy, and she wore the barest trace of lipstick and eye shadow. She hoped Latesha wouldn't tease her too much about that.

"Here," said David, holding out a white cardboard box. "This is for you."

Sarah took the box and pried off the top. Inside lay a delicate white flower, an orchid, she guessed.

"Oh, David, it's gorgeous!"

She lifted it gently out of the box and struggled to pin it on the shoulder of her dress. After two tries, pricking herself both times, she turned to David and appealed for help. He looked at her, at a loss.

"Here, let me help you."

Her mother came to the rescue. For once, Sarah was glad to have her interfere.

"Now why don't you two be on your way," she said to them as she stepped back to admire the corsage. "I wouldn't want you to miss any of the fun."

Sarah and David walked toward the car side by side, but not touching. Now that their date had officially begun, Sarah felt incredibly ill at ease. What was she supposed to do now? Should she wait for him to make the first move, reach for her hand, put his arm around her shoulder or waist? Or was she supposed to take the initiative? After all, she was a feminist. The old rules no longer applied, right? Oh, why hadn't she gone over these details with Latesha or Dominique last night? She felt like an absolute moron!

All the way to the restaurant where the prom was being held, neither of them spoke. They sat at opposite ends of the back seat, staring out the windows. David's father tried to make small talk, but gave up after a few minutes. Sarah was relieved when he turned on the radio.

When he dropped them off at the Hotel Chanticleer, he simply said goodbye and drove off. Sarah was impressed. Her own father would not have been so cool. He would have said something embarrassing like "Don't do anything I wouldn't do" or "Call me for a ride home if things get out of hand." David was lucky.

The night passed quickly. David and Sarah made a few feeble attempts to mingle with the others, but they didn't really want to be part of the crowd. They also didn't particularly like to dance. Instead, they sat on one of the plush couches in the corridor just outside the ballroom, sipping Cokes and talking. Occasionally, one of Sarah's classmates would walk by and make some snide remark like "All talk, no action," or "This is a prom, not a debating club."

But Sarah and David ignored them. In fact, they were discovering that they really had a lot in common. They both loved animals, liked to watch vampire movies, had a passion for Italian water ice. Sarah told David about her dreams of being a zookeeper. He told her about his plans to be a pediatrician. They talked about their families—about Mikey's disabilities and David's father's heart condition. No matter how long they talked, they never seemed to run out of things to say.

"Hey, you guys, it's time to go down the shore—if you can tear yourselves away from your blabbering!"

It was Tony Parker, with a smiling Latesha on one arm.

"Come on, Sarah, time to get the *real* prom going."

Sarah and David looked at each other. It was clear from their faces that neither wanted to go with the others, but there was no escape. Sarah knew that if she backed out now, she would never live it down.

The ninety teenagers piled into the two school buses rented by Springfield and set off for the Delaware shore. The back seats were crammed with duffel bags and knapsacks, holding bathing suits, towels, blankets, flashlights—and beer, although none of the chaperones knew about it.

During the ride, most of the couples kissed and groped in the dark. Sarah and David continued talking, but this time their conversation was driven by nervousness, not interest. Sarah felt tense and embarrassed, especially when one of the boys sitting in the seat behind them shouted, "Are you guys just *talking?*" The remark was followed by gales of laughter from the others. Sarah felt her cheeks burning.

Finally, they arrived at the beach and poured out of the bus, lugging their bags as they clambered toward the wooden steps leading to the dunes and the water's edge beyond. Within minutes, the beach came alive, as many exchanged evening clothes for bathing suits and ran into the surf. Standing at the wooden steps leading down to the beach, Sarah could just make out a few gleaming white bodies bobbing in the dark waves. The chaperones seemed to have disappeared.

David now walked up to Sarah, and slipped his hand around her waist.

"Let's take a walk, Sarah. It's a beautiful night."

Sarah thought she heard a change in his voice. He sounded nervous, unsure. Which was exactly how *she* felt with his arm around her now.

"Uh, are you sure we should, David? I mean, it's awfully dark, and we don't really know our way around this beach."

"Oh, come on, Sarah. You heard them on the bus. We can't just talk all the time."

She definitely didn't like the tone in his voice. Suddenly she felt afraid. Maybe all that talk back at the restaurant was a come-on. Maybe he was just softening her up for the kill.

"I don't think we should, David. I'd rather stay here with the others."

"What's the matter, Sarah? Afraid to enjoy yourself? You're only young once, you know."

His lines sounded like they'd been taken right out of some old movie. She tried to break free of his arm around her middle, but he tightened his grip.

"Come on. Loosen up, Sarah. Would I do anything to hurt you?"

Reluctantly, against her better judgment, Sarah let herself be led along the beach toward a row of low dunes. The moon and stars were now partially covered by clouds. David walked them steadily toward the dunes, and then behind them. Sarah felt a chill seeping into her bones. She shouldn't be here with him. What if he . . .

And then she felt his hands pressing against her cheeks, his mouth on hers. She tried to break free, but David wouldn't let her. He pushed her down onto the sand and began pulling at her dress, trying to push it off her shoulders. She struggled to pull away, to shout for help. David clamped one hand over her mouth and reached into his jacket with the other hand, pulling out a thin flask. He worked off the top with his forefinger and thumb, then took a long swig from the bottle. Almost immedi-ately, he began to choke, loosing his hold on Sarah's mouth.

"What the hell do you think you're doing, you creep!" she shouted. "I thought you were different. Boy, was I wrong!"

The pounding surf drowned out her voice so that she could hardly hear herself. But David clearly heard her. He stood shak-ing his head, and then sank down to his knees. Sarah started pounding him on the back and shoulders, crying and screaming at the same time.

"Stop it, Sarah!" David shouted, looking up at her. At that moment, the clouds parted, unveiling the shimmering moon. In the bright moonlight, Sarah saw David's eyes brimming with tears. She felt no pity for him.

"Please, Sarah," he continued shouting, "I'm sorry! I only did it because I was embarrassed by what they were saying about me. I didn't want them to think I was . . . you know, unmasculine or weird or something."

"I don't care what they think!" screamed Sarah, starting to walk back to the others. "If that's how you want to treat me, you can go to hell!"

David ran after her and grabbed her arm, stopping her flight. "I'm sorry, Sarah. I'll never do anything like that again. It was awful. Please give me another chance. Please!"

"Why should I?" countered Sarah, although she already felt her anger fading. She was no stranger to peer pressure herself.

"Because you're a good person, and you have a big heart," David said, smiling.

"Flattery will get you five more minutes," Sarah answered, smiling back. She scolded herself for being such a softie, but that was just the way she was. No use fighting it.

"OK, how about going back to the others, changing into bathing suits, and then going swimming? Hands off, honest! And," he drew the flask out of his jacket where he'd pocketed it, "no more of this stuff." He pulled back his arm and flung the bottle as hard as he could toward the white line of the ocean. They heard a faint splash as it landed in the surf.

"OK, David, you've got your second chance. But that's it. One wrong move and you're dead meat."

Laughing, they ran back to the area of beach now strewn with blankets and giggling couples. Two huge bonfires blazed on the beach, lighting up the sky. Latesha and Dominique hailed them as they came into view.

"Hey, where have you two been? Up to some mischief?" teased Latesha. "You disappeared for a long time."

"That's for us to know, and you to find out," answered Sarah, winking at David.

Dominique and Latesha looked at each other, raised their eyebrows, and then stared at Sarah, nodding. They motioned for her to follow them, leaving David still grinning by one of the large bonfires.

"OK, Eisenberg, 'fess up," commanded Latesha. "Did you do it or didn't you? And none of your doubletalk!"

"What do you think, Latesha?"

"I think I'd better mind my own business," laughed Latesha.

"And what about you and Tony?" asked Sarah.

"You can pry all you want," sighed Latesha. "Nothing to tell."

"Wish I could say the same for Chris," moaned Dominique.

The other two looked at Dominique with sympathy. She laughed. "Just kidding! He talks a good game, but it's all bluff."

The three girls began to laugh. They were soon laughing so hard that they fell over onto the sand and grabbed their sides to stop shaking. Suddenly, Latesha sprinted toward the water, shouting and waving her arms wildly. Screaming, the two others ran after her and plunged into the icy waves. When the three of them emerged from the surf moments later, the sun was already peeking over the dunes, turning the sky a brilliant pink.

It promised to be a perfect day.